Hidden Hurt

Kia Stokes

LOS ANGELES COUNTY, CALIFORNIA

KIA STOKES

Publisher's Note: This is a work of fiction. Names, characters, places, and incidents are a product of the author's imagination. Locales and public names are sometimes used for atmospheric purposes. Any resemblance to actual people, living or dead, or to businesses, companies, events, institutions, or locales is completely coincidental.

Hidden Hurt by Kia Stokes -- 1st ed.
ISBN: 978-1-949461-15-2

Dedication

This book is dedicated to all my girlfriends that have been on this amazing journey with me. Thanks for all the laughs, tears, prayers, waiting to exhale sleepovers, lemonade, chips, and salsa! LOL! ♥

Blank pages are intentional

TABLE OF CONTENTS

KIA STOKES

Hurt that is not revealed, is hurt that won't truly heal.

CHAPTER ONE

Just Another Day

It's another stormy day, and Alecia hadn't put the cover on the pool. It served her right for listening to the weatherman. They didn't know half of what they were talking about anyway. A dry day was definitely not promised during the springtime here in Chipley, Georgia, the most urban city in the state. Alecia, affectionately known as Lele by her girls, loved to listen to her classical music while sitting in her bedroom window. Three more months and her son Addonte' would be home from boarding school. If it weren't for church and her girlfriends, Shantel, Kim, and Monay, she would be crazy by now. Alecia was so lonely at times being there without Addonte.' He had only been gone two months, and that seemed like forever. She couldn't wait to hear him say, "Hello, Mother, I'm home!" Alecia only wished that he would say he was home permanently.

After she and Addai's divorce was final, Addonte' decided the best thing for him was to leave for a while. He suffered so much pain and embarrassment from what happened; he just needed a change of scenery. He wasn't the only one, though. If Alecia could leave, she would.

Alecia still felt so responsible for what happened to Addonte'. God has said to her repeatedly that she needed to forgive herself. She thanked God Addonte' was a mature twelve-year-old and he had forgiven her. Deep down, Alecia knew what happened wasn't her fault, but that still didn't take away the guilt. A mother is supposed to protect her children, and she failed him. Alecia just didn't think that she had to protect him from his own father. "What kind of sick pervert would rape a child repeatedly, let alone his own son? I should have recognized the changes in Addonte' though," Alecia said to herself. He had such a bubbly personality and outgoing spirit. Then suddenly, he went into a shell. He didn't want to have family dinner or go anywhere with Alecia and Addai. She couldn't understand why because they had always been such a loving, close-knit family.

Alecia was still in shock most days. She and Addai were childhood sweethearts that lived across the street from one another and were the best of friends. Once they entered high school, they dated. Alecia had loved him since they were 6 years old, so once he became her boyfriend, no one could tell her anything. Their parents got along well, and they all took family vacations together. After high school graduation, Addai went to law school, and Alecia went to medical school. They hated to be apart from each other, so they always met up at home for the holidays. During his last year of law school, he asked Alecia to marry him. She was ecstatic. They had a small ceremony shortly after. They wanted something big but couldn't really afford it because Alecia still had another year of medical school and residency to complete. It didn't matter anyway, because if she and Addai were there, the service would go on.

Upon graduation from school, Alecia immediately got a job working at Pearlie General Medical Center. Addai and a friend of his had begun their law practice. Life was perfect, so she thought. Five years passed, and they talked about starting a family. So Addai threw out all of his condoms and told Alecia he wanted them to go half on a baby. Alecia became pregnant in a matter of weeks. They both hoped and prayed that it would be a little girl. She wanted a shopping partner, and Addai wanted somebody else to spoil other than her.

When they had their sonogram, it turned out that they were having a boy. After the initial disappointment, everything was okay. They sold the house they were living in and built them a mini mansion in the country. They named their son Addonte', but they called him AD. God had given Alecia everything her little heart desired, and to her, life was good.

It was years later that Alecia's world got turned inside out in a way she couldn't fathom. She never expected to come home to the mess that she did.

Alecia came home early one day so she could surprise AD and take him to dinner for being inducted into the national honor society at school. She pulled in the garage as she normally did and noticed Addai was home too. She thought that was even better because they could go out as a family. That was something that they had little time to do anymore because of their hectic schedules. When Alecia walked in the house, she heard AD screaming to the top of his voice at his father. She could not imagine what the problem could be, so she hurried upstairs to his bedroom. What she saw with her very eyes was so detrimental. Alecia saw her husband she loved dearly, performing oral sex on their son. She asked him what the hell he was doing and ran over and slapped him. She grabbed AD, ran to her bedroom hysterical, and locked the door. She hugged AD so tight and told him she was sorry. The first thing she thought to do was to go under the mattress and get the gun. Alecia couldn't believe that bastard had been abusing her precious child. She told AD to stay in her room until she came back.

Alecia went throughout the house looking for Addai. He was downstairs lying on the kitchen floor, crying that he was sorry. She walked in and told him he was right, he was sorry, a sorry excuse for a human. Alecia kicked him and told him to get the hell out of her house before the paramedics came to take him out in a body bag. He cried for Alecia to stop beating him and just listen to him. He said that he was sick and needed help. She pointed the gun at him and told him to get out for the last time. He finally got up and went outside. She told him to come back later and that some of his clothes would be in their guest house for him to pick up. Alecia slammed the door and fell to her knees and cried out to God. She knew it had to be a nightmare. That was her husband, her best friend, and love of her life.

After a while, AD came downstairs and found her on the floor. He began apologizing, telling her he was sorry. She explained to him that none of that was his fault. Alecia and AD talked for hours that night. She told him to take a bath, and then she put him to bed. He told her that Addai had been having sex with him since his eleventh birthday. He would beg him not to do that, but Addai told him that was the way he was supposed to express his love for his son and to make him a man. Alecia could not believe what she was hearing.

"Still today, I did not see any of the warning signs," Alecia said to herself. She heard the phone ring and looked on the caller id and saw it was her girl Shantel calling. She was supposed to be coming over, even though it was storming outside.

****

"Hey, Shantel, what's up?" Alecia asked.

"Girl, I have been out here ringing the doorbell for five minutes. What in the world are you doing in there? I know you don't have a man over. Open the door," the voice said over the receiver.

Alecia opened the door and said, "Hey, girl, I'm sorry about that. I was sitting in the window thinking about my life. I didn't even hear the doorbell."

"That's fine, Lele. I'll let you slide this time. I only wish you weren't coming to the door because you had a man in here getting you some," Shantel laughed.

"What's going on with you, Ta?"

"Nothing much, girl. Nothing new anyway. I'm just so tired of going through the same old financial struggles with Gerome."

"Girlfriend, I know. It will get better, though. Y'all have been paying y'all tithes, so you just have to wait on God. Sometimes it appears to get worse before it gets better, but it does get better. No storms last always, not even the one that's outside now."

"Yea, easy for you to say Miss thang since you sittin' on RICH!" Shantel chuckled.

"Shantel, I resent that statement. I've worked extremely hard to get where I am today. Didn't anybody give me a thing. God has been merciful to me. After my divorce, I didn't think me and AD would make it, but we did. Anyway, you really should try supporting your man, instead of downing him all the time. You remember the song, stand by your man," Alecia said very firmly.

"Heifer, what do you mean? I support that Negro in everything he does. Even though every time it's a flop. When will we ever get some financial stability? I ain't even trying to be rich, but I'm just tired of the struggle," Shantel said sarcastically.

Alecia placed her hand on her hip and replied, "Yea, I guess your version of supporting him is, go ahead and do it fool, it ain't gon' work or I told yo old stupid self it wasn't going to work. Girl, with that kind of support, he will never make it."

After she said that, she knew Shantel would be pissed off. Shantel never took criticism or correction in a positive way. But oh well, somebody had to tell her the truth. "Besides, that's what friends are for. If you can't tell your friend the truth, then you're not truly a friend," she said to herself.

"You know what; it's time for me to go before I have to slap you again. You are supposed to be understanding and here you are taking his side. What kind of friend are you?"

"I am not taking anybody's side. Right is right and wrong is wrong. You go ahead and leave Shantel like you always do. Your problems are going right along with you. One thing that is for sure, you can't run from yourself. You need to pray and ask God to deliver you. Ever since we were little, you always said you weren't going to be like your mama, but look at yourself, girl. You are just like her, negative and abusive. When someone says or does something you don't like, you cut them off. When is the cycle going to come to a halt? Huh, when?" Alecia asked.

Shantel cried and laid her head on Alecia's shoulder.

"I know, Lele. I can't stand myself like this, either. I really don't know how to change. I'm praying for some deliverance, but it just seems like it won't come. Sometimes I think that God has forgotten about me. I look at y'all and it seems like we won't ever come up financially," she sobbed.

Alecia grabbed Shantel by her hand and hugged her tight. She knew sometimes something as simple as a hug could get you through the day.

"Shantel, girl, I promise it will get better. You just have to trust God and believe that He is faithful to His word. Girl, He is not like man, He can't lie."

"I know. I'm really trying to hold on, but I can feel myself slipping away."

"God is going to come through. Sometimes it just takes a little while.

I wish I had a husband, and it just hurts me to my heart to see you treat yours the way that you do. Gerome has a job, loves the Lord, and he is faithful. Girl, do you know how many women are praying and waiting on a man like that? You can't find a straight, faithful man these days to save your life. You have no choice but to wait on God. Ta, y'all might not have all the money you all desire right at this moment, but at least you are on the right track. Can I just get a man?" Alecia laughed trying to make Ta smile. "You should consider the catering business that Gerome wants to start."

"Thanks, Lele, I needed that laugh. Girl, you'll get a man soon," Shantel giggled. "I'm going to go home and get myself together. I'll see you later for girl's night out. Thanks, so much for telling me the truth. Even though I don't like it, I can appreciate that. I don't know about the catering service. Everything we start turns out to be a flop. Love you, girl," Shantel said, heading out of the door.

"Love you too, chick. See you later," Alecia said, and the phone rang.

"Hello."

"Hey, girl, what time are we meeting tonight?"

"Hey, Kim, girl. Shantel just walked out of the door. I guess about sevenish. We are meeting at your house, so I hope you've already gotten permission from your hubby. I don't want us to be outside in the rain trying to fellowship," Alecia replied.

"Yea, girl, I have. James is going to meet Gerome at Winghut. I'm going to have to pick Monay silly self up, though. You know that's the only way she will show up. We can't depend on her for nothing."

"Right right." Alecia laughed in agreement and continued. "Ok, well, I'll see you then." Before Alecia could hang up the receiver, she heard Kim still talking.

"Wait, Lele. I almost forgot," Kim said.

"Yea, Kim, you almost forgot what?" she asked.

"We know you are tired of us trying to play matchmaker with you, but I have this dude for you to meet tonight. He is not like all of the other ones, okay. So, make sure you're looking cute."

"Girl, now you know I am through playing the hookup game with you. Forget it. I do not have time to raise these little boys up to be men. That's what their mommas were for.

"Come on, Lele. You have to trust me this time. I am for real, chick. He's saved and everything. Can you at least meet him?"

"Nope, now goodbye. I have to make the rotel," she said and slammed the phone.

"That girl is crazy," Alecia said to herself. Alecia did want a man, but Kim thought she was desperate. She was tired of always ending up at a dead end with a blind date. Alecia was interested in having a friend to talk to and wondered what would it hurt just to say hello? "Lord, if this guy means me no good, then don't even allow me to meet him. My husband will never find me if I don't even allow myself to meet anybody."

CHAPTER TWO

Girl's Night Out

When Lele arrived at Kim's house, she saw Shantel's car parked in the driveway. So that should have meant everybody was there. That was a good thing because she was hungry and ready to hang out with her girls. She walked to the door and knocked.

"Knock knock knock in there. Is anybody home?" Lele yelled

Kim opened the door and told her to hush up disturbing her neighbors. Alecia walked in, and Shantel was kicked back on the couch with her shoes off.

"Hey, again, Shantel. Kim, what happened to you picking up Monay, or is she in the mirror somewhere?" Alecia looked around for her.

"Girl, I went by her house and she didn't answer. Her car and another car were under the carport, though. I figured it was one of her men," explained Kim.

"Which one?" Shantel said and everyone laughed.

"I don't know why Monay is loose and in clubs so much, but we just have to continue to pray for one another that we all might be healed. She's our friend, and she needs our help. So let's not talk about her since she is not here to defend herself," Lele said.

"Yea, whatever, Le. Ain't none of us sick, we don't need no healing," Shantel laughed.

"Girl, please, we all need healing in some area of our lives. Only God knows and you know too. Don't get me started on you, missy."

"Le, we all have had our issues, but we got our healing. I know I got mine," said Shantel.

"Okay, y'all keep thinking that. We are just going to pray that God reveals to us the areas where we need healing. Sometimes we think that we are alright and we're not. There is a reason for all of our actions and…"

Before Lele could finish her mini sermonette, the doorbell rang.

"Whew, saved by the bell. I did not feel like hearing another sermon," Kim said.

Kim opened the door and in walked Monay trying to hug everybody.

"Hey, y'all. Sorry I'm late. I had to handle a little business before I came. I can't stay long, either. Froggies is having free drinks tonight for the ladies. Y'all can join me if y'all want to. Lele, you know there will be plenty of men there for you, honey."

"Girl, now you know we are not going to a club, and you need to keep your butt out of there too. I definitely don't want anything that's hanging out in a club, and especially at Froggies," Lele said.

"And what kind of business you had to handle that was more important than us? I came by your house and saw another car there hoochie," Kim explained.

"Okay, okay, okay. That was my new man. I met him last week at Froggies. He is so fine. He owns an engineering company and ain't got no kids. Even better than that, he don't want none, just like me. The Lord really blessed me this time. I think we gon' get married this summer after he gets a divorce. Don't y'all get started talking about him cheating on his wife, because it ain't cheating. He is just having an extramarital adventure," Monay said with excitement.

Shantel shook her head in disbelief and said, "Monay, shut up, girl."

Everybody knew that the talk about children always made Kim sad because she was having so many problems trying to conceive.

"Oops, I'm sorry, Kim. I know how bad you want some babies. Don't listen to me."

Kim bowed down her head and tears rolled down her face. "It's ok, I'm alright. It's my own fault I don't have any children."

"Kim, it is not your fault that you were raped. So stop beating yourself up," Shantel said.

"Yea, I hear you. It's just so hard sometimes not to think that I didn't cause all of this heartache and pain. Every time I see how bad James wants children; it just breaks my heart. But anyway, y'all give me some tissue. I'm okay. Let's have some fun," Kim cried.

Kim and her husband had been trying to conceive for 9 years. Kim was raped years prior, and her husband thought that because of the trauma, she couldn't get pregnant. Kim hadn't been completely honest with him, though.

"So Monay, you just met the guy last week, and you are sleeping with him already? I have told you about your loose behind. You are going to end up with something penicillin can't cure if you keep on. You are just like a child because the more I preach to you the worse you get," Lele fussed.

"Girl, yea. Are you crazy? He has been showering me with gifts since we met. You see this new bracelet he got me from Tiffany's? He is so sweet, and, girl, that sex is off the chain! You know that's how I hook me a man. I have to give him something that will make him sweat in his sleep! Besides, he has to make a deposit on this nukee," Monay laughed.

"Monay, girl, you are so stupid. Those men are only using you for your body. You should want better for yourself," Lele said.

"Yep, and I am just using them for their money, so it equals out. You've been to college. You should know that it's called bartering."

"All y'all really make me think twice about getting remarried," laughed Lele.

"Whatever holy roly. Where is the food? I can't be drinking on an empty stomach."

"It's some rotel, meatballs, hot wings, and tuna in the kitchen. Help yourself trifling," Kim said to Monay.

"Tuna?! I definitely can't have that trying to meet a man. Are y'all trying to mess up my game or something?" Monay yelled.

"Lord, please help that girl. I thought you would marry the dude you just left. You are so unstable, girl," Alecia said.

"Well, I ain't married yet. I am not sure when I am going to propose to him, though," Monay giggled.

After that comment, everyone laughed and headed to the kitchen to fix their food. Alecia always loved being with her girlfriends. No matter what she was going through, every time they got together, it didn't matter anymore that she was all alone.

"Lele, I have a question. Promise you won't get an attitude," Shantel said.

"Here we go. Ok, Ta, what is it?" Alecia sighed.

"Why did you really get a divorce? You've never really told us anything but that you made a mistake. I know there is more to it than that as long as y'all were together. So, what happened? Did he beat you or cheat on you?" Shantel inquired.

Alecia paused and took a deep breath. She was still not ready to discuss her divorce yet. "Why did Shantel have to open her big mouth?" Lele thought.

"I am not ready to talk about it yet. It's still very painful and hard for me to discuss," Lele said, praying that Shantel let it go.

"What?! You not ready? I thought we didn't have any secrets. Girl, and you are the main one around here talking about we need healing; you should be the first one in the healing line. You need to sit on the mourners' bench," Shantel said, and everyone laughed. "It must be really bad, though, because you give every man you meet, a very hard time."

"I've never denied that I need healing because I know I do. And I just don't want to make the same mistake twice. I thought I was so sure the first time," Lele explained.

Shantel laughed and replied, "Talking about your pain is the first step to healing. I do know that much."

"Shantel, just leave it alone. She'll talk about it when she gets ready. Let's move on to the next subject," Kim said. Kim was the peacemaker in the group.

Before anybody else could say anything, the doorbell rang. The girls sat with a confused look on their faces. They wondered who that could be because they all were already there. Kim got up to go answer the door while the girls continued to eat.

****

"Hey, Darryl. Glad you could make it. Come on in," Kim said and hugged the guy standing in the door.

"Hey, Kim. Glad you invited me. Am I late?" Darryl asked.

"Of course not. You are right on time."

"Good. Which one is she? I am ready to meet her. This could be the lady for me."

Kim led Darryl to the living room and said, "Hey, everybody, this is Darryl. He stopped by to work on my computer. This is Monay, Shantel, and this is Alecia, but everyone calls her Lele."

"Hello, ladies, it's nice to meet all of you, especially you, Alecia," Darryl said in a flirtatious manner heading to Kim's office.

"Whew! Especially you, Alecia. What was that all about? Lele, looks like someone finds you attractive. You better get him, girl. Get him, get him! He's HOT!" Monay shouted.

"Yea, Lele, why don't you go and ask him a computer question. That is your little hobby ya know," Shantel said, trying to convince Lele to approach Darryl.

Lele turned to the girls and demanded them to please stop with the jokes. "It's not even like that. He is a nice-looking guy, but that does not mean a thing. Didn't we just talk about me getting my healing?

Would y'all just let me be? When God sees fit for me to have a husband, I will."

"Yeah, y'all, just leave miss holier than thou alone," Kim giggled.

Everybody laughed and Kim pulled out Guesstures. Guesstures was a game they played every time they got together. It was so much fun watching how creative they all were when acting out the words on the cards.

"Well, Lele, if you don't want him, I'll turn him out tonight before I go to the club!" Monay joked.

"That's your problem now, Monay. You need to stop sleeping with every man you see. You are such a little whore," Shantel said.

"A whore? Listen here, you little husband beater, you better stop talking to me now. Don't get me started on you," Monay rolled her eyes.

"Alright y'all, that is enough. Back to you, Lele. Girl, why won't you open up or won't allow anyone to get close to you? You really might want to get some counseling from your divorce," Kim asked out of concern for her friend.

"Y'all I really do appreciate the concern, but look, can we talk about something else. What do y'all think about the choir? I was considering joining next month," Alecia said quickly, trying to change the subject. "What did I say that for?" she thought to herself. Everybody burst out laughing at her.

"Alecia Mondrake, you already on every board at the church. You need to try joining me at the club," Monay said sarcastically.

After Monay made her little joke, Darryl walked in from Kim's office. Darryl was a nice-looking man. He was about six feet tall with a muscular build. His skin was so smooth and dark it reminded Alecia of a piece of Hershey's dark chocolate. A smile so sweet and his teeth were perfectly lined and white. Darryl's nails were so clean and filed for a man. He had to have his nails professionally done. "I sure wouldn't mind getting to know him. No, what is wrong with me? Lord, I cast down these wicked imaginations," Alecia thought to herself.

"Excuse me, ladies, I don't mean to interrupt. I was just going to throw away a computer part, but I couldn't help but hear you all's conversation. Alecia, I think you should join the choir. I would love to come and hear you sing sometimes too. You have a beautiful speaking voice, so I know it would be angelic to hear a song come from you," Darryl said.

"My, it's getting a little too hot in here for me. I'll holla at y'all tomorrow. I'm headed to Froggies. Goodbye, Mr. Darryl," Monay smirked and pinched Darryl's cheek.

"She ain't nothing but an old slut," Shantel laughed.

"Thanks for the compliment, Darryl. That was really sweet. I'll be sure that Kim let you know if I do join," Alecia smiled at Darryl.

Darryl must have been as nervous as Alecia was because he was over there sweating. Kim and Shantel were over in the corner laughing. They were such silly girls. Alecia hoped they were over there praying for her, though, because she hadn't talked to a man in so long, she didn't want to say anything wrong.

"So, I hear you're into computers," Darryl commented.

"Now I wonder how you heard that. Yea, I was. I don't really have time to deal with them too much now, though," Alecia replied.

"Well, Alecia, I don't mean to come off so strong, but can I call you sometimes or take you out to dinner tomorrow night?"

Alecia stood with a blank look on her face. "What should I say?" As soon as that thought ran through her mind, she heard Kim and Shantel coughing loud in the background. "I guess that means to say yes," Alecia thought.

"Darryl, you are quite charming, I must say, but I don't think so. I just really don't have time for games," said Alecia.

"Who said anything about games? I just want to get to know you. Alecia, that is not a crime or a sin. Come on, give me a chance. I don't bite."

"Okay, Darryl. It is just dinner. Besides, if I don't say yes, Kim and Shantel will be hoarse from all of that coughing. Here, I will put my number in your phone. Please don't call me after nine, unless it is an emergency."

Darryl was so elated that Alecia told him yes, that he jumped in the air and clicked his heels together.

"You have made my night. I hope I am not blushing too hard. I'll call you tonight so we can finalize some plans. Can you be ready for dinner by 6:00? I don't want to have you out too late since we both have to get up for church service the next day."

"Sure, I will be ready at 5:45 just in case you come early. You be sure to drive safely on your way home. I'll talk to you later. I guess I can show you some leniency to call me after hours tonight since I'll be here a little while longer," said Alecia, then plopped down on the couch. You could tell she was trying extremely hard not to scream. Alecia was excited, but she couldn't let him know that.

"Well, goodnight, ladies. Once again, it was nice meeting all of you. Kim, I'll be talking to you."

"I'll walk you out, Darryl," Kim said and continued. "Yes, I am so happy." Kim sighed.

"Thanks, Kim. I owe you, girl. Alecia is beautiful and has such a peaceful spirit."

In the living room, Shantel was going wild. She appeared to be more excited than Lele was. Shantel was hollering and jumping up and down. Then Kim headed over.

"Lele got a man! Praise the God you serve," Shantel yelled.

"Yes, God. I am too thrilled. Girl, what are you going to wear tomorrow? You know I have clothes in the closet with tags on them if you need to go and grab you something. Please dress cute and not like you are going to church with a long Holy Ghost skirt on," Kim laughed.

"Would y'all please calm down? I don't have a man yet. We are just going to dinner, dang. Y'all won't even give me time to get my thoughts together," Lele said sternly.

"Girl, please. He is all into you, Lele. He really is a good saved guy. Just please take the wall down and give him a chance," Kim pleaded.

"Lele whatever. So, what are you going to wear?" Shantel asked.

"I don't even know and would y'all put your breaks on? It's not like we're getting married tomorrow. I am not getting my hopes up high this time. Whatever God allows to happen, that's what will happen. We may just become best buds or something. Kim, pass me my drink," Lele said.

"Girl, I am not passing anything. The party is over. Lele, you need to go home and find something to wear and talk to the Lord on your way home. I already know you are going to pray. Just remember, everything happens for a reason. Now, y'all get out. James should be home momentarily."

"Forget both of y'all. Just let me get my shoes on," said Lele.

"Well, be sure you call me as soon as the date is over. I'll be waiting by the phone," Shantel laughed.

As Lele pulled out of Kim's driveway, she saw James about to pull in. She blew her horn and drove away.

****

James walked in the house and hugged Kim.

"Hey, boo, I have something for you. He hands her flowers. Oh, you are so warm. How did your little cupid scheme go?" James said and passionately kissed Kim.

"Thanks for my flowers, sweetie. You are so thoughtful. My little scheme went perfectly! Cupid's arrow hit them both straight in the heart," she chuckled. "Boyyyyy, they are going out tomorrow. I don't even think Lele realized that's who I wanted to hook her up with. God is just good like that. I'll tell her about everything later," Kim said.

"Baby, you are something else with yourself. That's why I love you so much."

"So, what did you and Gerome do other than eat too much at Winghut?" Kim asked.

James sat up with a strange look and said, "Nothing much. He was just talking about him and Shantel. Gerome said that your girl needs some serious counseling. Y'all need to talk to your friend. He said she does not fight him as much as she used to, but she is just so darn angry all of the time. He said it's like walking around the house on eggshells. The brother can't say or do anything wrong or Shantel turns into someone else. She got like three or four different spirits, split personalities he says."

"Boo, we are praying and fasting with her. Lele has been trying to talk to her a lot more too. At least she has gotten a little better. Shantel really does want to change, so she will get delivered. I just hope Gerome can be patient with her during this process," Kim explained.

"Well, that girl needs an exorcism," James laughed.

Kim burst out laughing and said, "Boy, you are too stupid. I love you. Now that was too funny. So, what are we going to do tomorrow? It has been so long since we have had a Saturday with nothing to do."

"Tomorrow will take care of itself," James said and leaned in to kiss her. "What are we going to do tonight?"

Kim giggled like a high school kid. James always kept a smile on her face. "Let's see what we can come up with, my tiger man. Come here."

****

SHANTEL'S HOUSE

Shantel hoped Gerome was awake when she arrived home. She couldn't wait to tell him that Lele had a date. When she walked in the house, she heard him laughing, so she knew he was up watching television.

"Hey, honey, I see you made it home alright. I saw a wreck on the highway on my way home," Shantel said.

"Yea, I have been here for a few minutes. I'm just sitting here watching a little Good Times. How was girls' night?" Gerome asked.

"Baby, it was off the chain as usual. Monay left going to the club to meet a man, and Lele has a date. Can you believe it? I can't remember the last time she went out on a date. Kim had a friend of hers to stop by to pretend to fix her computer, just so he could meet Lele. Lele don't even have a clue that it was all planned," she laughed.

"Well, that's good for her. Do you feel like talking?"

"Now what does he want to talk about? Things have gotten better, so he has nothing to complain about. I've had a really good night and I really, I mean really, don't feel like ruining the rest of it," Shantel wondered.

"Uh oh. What's wrong now, Gerome? I've had a good night and I really don't feel like fussing. This is not a good time. Let's just go take a hot shower and go to bed, okay," she said in a seductive manner.

"Shantel, it's always something. No time is ever a good time. If we don't ever address our issues and try to get some help, we are not going to make it. Baby, listen to me," Gerome said with tears flowing.

It was often hard for Gerome to express himself without crying. He was a very emotional and sensitive person.

"I love you and you are the only one for me, but I can't live like this anymore. I know you don't hit me anymore, but your attitude is so bad, and you talk to me like I am a nobody.

You constantly put me down and make me feel like nothing that I do for you is good enough. I am no longer going to accept this abuse from the person that is supposed to love me. We are either going to get some counseling, or we are going to have to go our separate ways. I really want our marriage to work, but this is not healthy for either of us, or especially not the girls."

When Gerome spoke, Shantel's tears just flowed. It hurt her so bad to see him cry like that.

"Gerome, I know I need some help. I have been praying for God to change me, but I just don't know how to change. I am sorry that I take all of my frustrations out on you. Please help me. I don't want to lose you, my family, or my sanity. These childhood demons have just about taken over my life. I just don't know what to do. What do I do?" Shantel screamed.

Shantel fell to her knees in despair. She could feel Gerome kneel down beside her. He gently placed his arm around her and just held her. He stroked her hair, prayed and cried out like a newborn. After minutes of crying and praying, he lifted Shantel from the floor and sat her on his lap. Gerome knew she loved to sit on his lap because she didn't have an opportunity to do that as a child.

"Shantel, this is the first time after 13 years that you have acknowledged that you need help. God will honor that, and I do too. Confession is the first step to receiving your healing. I love you, boo, and I just don't want you to allow your past to ruin our present and future. The children need two stable parents. I can't be mother and father anymore. I know things are not going to change overnight but over time. I am willing to work with you. I love you more than you'll ever know," Gerome exclaimed.

"Thanks so much, Gerome. You really don't know how much your love and compassion mean to me. I guess you gon' make me fast too, huh? I'm just kidding, honey," Shantel laughed.

"Okay now. Girl, you know some demons only prayer and fasting can get rid of," Gerome giggled. "I know a good counselor for us to go to. His name is Dr. TL Roberts and he has been a marriage counselor for 35 years.

His track record of keeping marriages together is quite impressive. I could probably get us an appointment on your day off."

"Well, babe, it really doesn't matter who we see as long as they make house visits. I really don't think I can handle going to a public office. I would like to be counseled in the privacy of our own home," she said.

"You know what? I think he does. I will call him on Monday, baby, and make sure, though. I'll also see what I can set up for next week. Now, sweetie, I have a question for you. Do you make house calls?" Gerome said seductively.

"Yes, I do, but I am expensive. How much are you willing to pay?" Shantel smirked and kissed Gerome.

****

LELE'S HOUSE

"Alecia, I can't believe we have been on the phone for three hours," Darryl said.

"I know. It has been a long time since I have even talked to a guy on the phone, let alone for three hours. You have good conversation," Alecia said, and then she noticed her other line was ringing. "Now who is that calling me at this time of the night? Can you hold on for a minute, Darryl?"

"Hello?" she said in a frustrated tone.

"Hey, Lele, girl, I heard you got a date tomorrow. I'm going to come over and pick out your outfit and do your makeup. We do not want you looking like an old maid," Monay laughed.

"Monay, what do you want at 2:00 in the morning? I have told y'all about calling me all time of the night. I know you aren't still at the club," Lele replied.

"Girl, I am leaving now. I'm headed to this guy's house that I just met. He is so fine, and he drives a Mercedes coupe. Anyway, why do you sound like you are awake anyway? What are you doing?"

"Girl, I am just up, lying here in the bed. I'll talk to you tomorrow," Lele said, trying to rush Monay off of the phone.

"Lele, you know you don't know how to lie good. You are not up praying because if you were, you wouldn't have answered the phone. I know you don't have a man over there. What is your little sneaky self-doing?" Monay questioned.

"Okay, okay, but you better not blab your big mouth to anybody else. I am on the phone talking to Darryl and, girl, we have been on the phone for the past three hours. So, I am really going to have to let you go," she screamed with excitement.

"What? No ma'am. Girl, you are finally about to get you some after all of these years. Remember when you let him get it, please use a condom," Monay laughed. "My holy roly friend is about to get laid. Your vibrator days are coming to an end."

"Bye, Monay. I'll talk to you tomorrow. Love ya, girl," Lele said and hung up in her face. Alecia immediately clicked back over to Darryl. "Hey, Darryl, sorry about that.

That was Monay crazy self that you met over at Kim's house. She is just leaving the club. Pray much for her."

"Oh, okay, because I started to wonder about you receiving calls this time of the morning. Especially, when you told me from the door not to call you after nine," Darryl said.

"Excuse me, mister?" Lele questioned with a humongous smile on her face. She thought it was so cute that he would call her out so quickly.

"Well, I can't have anybody disrespecting my wife's house and all. If I can't call, definitely can't anybody else call," said Darryl trying to lay down the law. She really couldn't believe he said that. She found it rather flattering, though. "I am not your wife. I am married to the Lord. You don't even know me boy."

"You're right, I don't know everything about you. But my relationship with the Lord is real and I know what he told me. I am not going to pressure you into anything, and we are just going to take it day by day," Darryl said in confidence.

"Okay, whatever, Darryl. So, are you still not going to tell me where we are going to eat? I want to kind of have in my mind what I will eat."

"No, ma'am, I am not. Just relax and wait until we get there. You cannot know everything. Are you still not going to tell me why you got a divorce?" Darryl asked, trying to get smart.

"Darryl, I've told you that I'll tell you later. My friends don't even know that about me, and we are joined at the hip. How would it look with me telling a complete stranger? Besides, does it make a difference anyway?"

"No, it doesn't make a difference. I just want to know everything about the person I will spend the rest of my life with, that's all."

"Boy, would you stop saying that? It's about time for us to hang up and go to bed anyway. I have a hair appointment at eight and then I still have to find something to wear. So, I'll talk to you tomorrow," Lele explained.

"Yea, you're right. I'm over here yawning myself. Do you need any money to get your hair done? I can drop it off for you if you need me to."

"No, I don't, thanks. You sure are moving pretty fast, buddy."

"I just want to make sure you're taken care of. You'll soon find out that I am a very giving person. You know God can't bless you when you're selfish. Where do you get your hair done?" Darryl asked.

"I go to Imagi Beauty and Barber salon over on Towne Center Blvd. My friend Torri owns it. It's really nice. She has a nail technician and a massage therapist on site too. I told her she should get a full-service spa added," she replied.

"Oh, okay. Well, sweetie, you go ahead and get to bed. I'll pick you up about 5:30."

"Wait before you go. I know my son is not home, but I don't like people to know where I live. I did just meet you and all. Is it okay if you pick me up from Kim's house?" She didn't want him to think she was a weirdo or anything, but he could have been a mass murderer.

He should understand, though. Alecia was a wealthy single black female that lived alone. She couldn't just take chances with every Bob, Hank, and Candiman knowing where she lived.

"Sure, whatever you want. I'll see you at Kim's at 5:30. I'll call her and make sure it's alright. Goodnight, dumpling."

"Goodnight," she said smiling. "Lord, what is really going on? I feel like this is so right, but I don't even know him. He is so caring and has such a sweet spirit. He has his own business, he's saved, no children, never been married, and he's stable. Then on top of that, he said he is extremely close to his mother and sisters. He's everything I have written on my list Lord. I surely don't want to get all excited for another letdown, though. Then on the other hand, if I don't give this a chance, I will never know what will come out of it. I guess I'll just have to take a chance. If it works out, fine, and if it doesn't, oh well, for him. It will definitely be his loss. "Lord, I need you to shield my heart and help me to receive this man if he is my husband," Lele thought to herself.

CHAPTER THREE

Full of Surprises

lecia lay in bed, sleeping when the phone rang. She rolled over to look at the clock, and it read six o'clock a.m. She wondered who would be calling her that early in the morning, and especially on a Saturday morning. Alecia thought that the person calling had better have an emergency. She lifted her mask from her face and answered the phone.

"Hello," Alecia said with bass in her voice.

"Good morning, beautiful. It's me, Darryl."

Alecia could not believe Darryl was calling her that early in the morning. That gesture sure did manage to put a big smile on her face, though. "I better clear up my throat before I run him off," she thought.

"Good morning, Darryl. You're up rather early. Is everything alright?" Alecia asked, trying to figure out why he was calling her so early.

"Yes, everything is great. First, I wanted to apologize for not ending our conversation in prayer last night. I don't want to make the same mistake twice. So, are you ready for morning devotion?"

"You say you want to do what? Morning devotion?" she asked in a state of disbelief. Alecia was so surprised yet happy. She jumped up out of the bed and shouted. She glanced over at her prayer list and noticed she missed something. "Now I didn't even have sense enough to have that on my list and God is giving it to me anyway. Ain't nothing like a man that can lead his family in prayer," she thought to herself. Alecia settled herself down and continued, "Yes, Darryl, I'm ready."

Darryl prayed.

"In Jesus name, Amen," Alecia agreed.

"Okay, I'm going to let you lay back down. Get some breakfast on your way to the shop. Breakfast is the most important meal of the day," Darryl said.

"I probably won't have time. I'll grab something afterward. But let me go so I can jump in the shower. I'll call you after I leave the salon," Alecia said.

"Okay, beautiful. I'll be waiting on your call."

After Darryl hung up from Alecia, he called his brother to ask him for a favor.

****

Alecia pulled up at the shop and noticed that she was the first one there. The only other cars she saw belonged to the barbershop side. She knew Torri was always late and that she would be pulling up any minute. On the mornings she came, she usually called Torri at home to make sure she was awake. Torri had gotten much better recently, though. She's usually about ten minutes late. So, Alecia arrived at her appointment ten minutes after her scheduled time. That way, she wouldn't be sitting there looking crazy. She used to go on in and sit, but the guys getting their hair cut were too loud. To her, it sounded like they were having an early morning party. "I'll just sit here and listen to my cd," she thought.

Jesus is my rock and my salvation…
Who shall I fear…

God is the strength of my life...
That's why, you have to draw near...
Near to him where peace abide...
Joy unspeakable now reside...

While Alecia was singing her song, she saw Torri pulling up. She got out of her platinum Infiniti truck and headed towards the door. She heard Torri hollering with her normal slogan, 'girl you know I'm sorry. I'm going to do better.' Alecia threw her hand up as always, letting her know whatever! She walked in the salon and went straight to Torri's chair. "I am in desperate need of a relaxer and Mizani is my best friend. My hair is so thick; I can't even feel my scalp. I just took some micro braids out a couple of days ago. I know Torri is going to talk about me, because every time I've had braids, I always break one of her combs," she thought to herself.

"So, Torri, what have you and Jon been up to lately? You know it's been a while since I have been here," Alecia asked.

"Girl, nothing new. Me, him and the kids just came back from our third vacation this year. Jon just got weekends off at the hospital and we have been keeping the road hot. You are my only customer today. I took the rest of the day off, so I can get some sleep. So, what about you? Do you have a man yet?" Torri questioned.

"Well, actually, yes and no."

"Lele, what's yes and no? It's either one or the other boo."

"Well, I actually met a guy last night at Kim's house. It was almost as if he came there looking just for me. We stayed on the phone for a little over three hours last night. Girl, then he called me this morning for prayer. And we have a date tonight. So, I will say I have a friend," she answered with excitement.

"What?! He called you for prayer? Now, Lele, he is a keeper. You can't find that these days nowhere. It's like looking for a grain of rice in a haystack," Torri laughed.

"Girl, I know. I hadn't had a praying man since my divorce," she said, looking out of the window. "Torri, who is getting some flowers?"

"What are you talking about?" Torri asked.

"TNT's Flower shop van just pulled up next to your car."

"Hmph, I don't know. It must be for somebody on the other side. Come on back to the shampoo bowl. Let me unlock the door so he can come on in," Torri said.

Alecia sat down at the shampoo bowl and propped her feet up on the stool. As soon as she laid her head back, she heard Torri yelling her name.

"What in the world is wrong with her hollering like somebody is attacking her?" she thought to herself. Alecia jumped up, forgetting that the stool was there and almost fell flat on her face. She was almost down the hallway when Torri said, "Girl, these flowers are for you! You got food too."

Alecia couldn't believe her eyes or ears. She saw the flower guy coming toward her with a huge bouquet of pink and green tulips in a beautiful green vase. There had to be about 20 balloons attached too. When he finally moved the flowers away from his face, she didn't believe her eyes then. The guy looked just like Darryl but taller.

He extended his hand out to shake Alecia's and said, "Alecia, these are for you. I can tell by the way you are staring at me that my brother did not tell you he had a twin. It's nice to meet you and I am Derrell. Darryl asked me to deliver these flowers, balloons, and this breakfast to you. He hopes you enjoy it."

Alecia did not believe Darryl kept that from her. There she was standing looking dumbfounded with perm in her hair.

"It's nice to meet you, Derrell, and no, I didn't know Darryl had a twin. Darryl is such a sweetheart. You are nice yourself getting up this early to deliver this," she said with a smile.

"Oh, it was no problem. My wife and I own the business. I will let you all get back to what you all were doing. It was nice meeting you, Alecia, and I hope to see you soon for family dinner," Derrell said and walked out of the door.

Alecia was astonished, just plain speechless. She leaned in to smell her flowers before she put everything down. They were so beautiful, and that breakfast smelled so good. "Torri, come on and get this perm out of my head so I can eat my breakfast my MAN sent me," she said with a loud voice. Then she realized she had just said, 'My MAN.' She knew she must have been really excited.

"Yo man? I thought you didn't have a man. Are those from the guy that you just met yesterday?" Torri asked in disbelief.

"Girl, yes, it is. Can you believe that? I can't. I did know that it was something different about him. Girl, that just made my day. I feel like such a princess. I have been waiting and praying for so long and this might be it. I know it's soon, but God can bless suddenly, right? When it's His will, it doesn't take long. I think I am just going to let God be who He is and work everything out in my favor."

"Lele, I hope this works out for you. You so deserve to be happy," Torri said as they headed back to her chair.

"I still can't believe Darryl didn't tell me he had a twin. It probably just slipped his mind, though. Torri needs to hurry up and throw these rollers in my hair. I am ready to get under the dryer, eat, and get home so I can call my girls. They are going to be screaming and trying to go to the bridal shop tomorrow. I already have my wedding planned out on paper in faith. I learned that from the girls, well, everybody except Monay. God said write the vision and make it plain. All I need to do is insert my Boaz name in the proper place and we can go forth in Jesus name," she said to herself.

****

After Alecia left the shop, she stopped at Ginger's Boutique and picked up the cutest black dress to wear with her strappy sandals. She arrived home around two in the afternoon. She got out with her lovely tulips and balloons. She was especially impressed that he bought her tulips. Tulips were once used as money because they were so highly valued. To Alecia, that told her he considered her to be of high value to him. She tried to call Darryl earlier to tell him thanks, but she didn't get an answer. "I guess I will have to thank him when I see him tonight," she thought. She called Kim to tell her about her sweet surprise and the first thing out of her mouth was 'Lele is about to get married.' Then she called

Shantel and Monay on three-way. They were excited, of course. They acted as if Jesus had been raised from the dead again. All three of the girls would be there to get Alecia ready for her date. She knew that would be a very interesting time.

Alecia didn't have too much time left, so she went to jump in the shower. She had taken a long hot bubble bath earlier that morning, but she needed to freshen up for her date. She told Kim she would be there around four so they could work a miracle on her. Knowing them, they would have a list of do's and don'ts for her to follow.

****

When Alecia arrived at Kim's house, everyone was already there.

"Okay, y'all, I'm here," she said, and they had a group hug.

"Lele, come on. We don't have that much time and you are in need of a miracle. With the man giving you surprises like that; you have to look your best.

There's no telling what he will do tonight," Monay laughed.

Lele sat on the stool in the bathroom and Monay whipped out her duffle bag of make-up. Kim was moisturizing her feet, hands, and legs, while Shantel touched up her hair. Lele felt like she was in her very own private studio to prepare for her next taping. Although she was excited, she knew she still had to pray that God would shield her heart. This is how so many women get hurt time and time again. We meet a man, he shows us a little attention, buy us a happy meal, and we fall head over heels in love. Soon after, the real man shows up and we get hurt yet again. Not that the real man wasn't there all along, but we just fail to acknowledge the signs being shown to us because we are so desperate and needy. I so thank God he delivered me out of that way of thinking. I desire to have a husband again, but if God decides not to give me one, I am happy with Jesus alone. But I surely do pray there is a husband for me in His will.

"Ok, Lele, stand up so you can slip into this dress. Kim, slip her sandals on and tie them up.

Shantel, get the camera and my Kia' perfume out of my purse," Monay demanded as if she was in charge.

"Lele, I can't believe you picked out this cute dress! It's just the right style and length. It hits right above the knee," Kim laughed.

"Oh, now don't act like the only thing I can wear are scrubs and church suits, sweetie," Lele said, and the doorbell rang.

Lele's heart raced as if that was going to be her first date since she's been on the earth. Kim went to answer the door while Monay and Shantel inspected Lele up and down and told her she looked hot. They said a little prayer and were off to the front. As they headed down the hall, Kim came walking fast with a huge smile on her face.

"Girl, Darryl sent a car to pick you up! Can you believe that? Here is the note from the chauffeur," Kim said with excitement.

"What does it say? Girl, open it up!" said Monay.

Lele opened the note, and it read, "Just because you're you, you're invited to, a fulfilling night of pleasure, friendly love, and romance; to start us off, can I have this dance? -Darryl"

Lele had a humongous grin on her face. Her girls were jumping and laughing.

"Y'all this man is so romantic. Lord, give me strength not to fall in so deep and out of my panties so quick in Jesus name. Girls, let me go, I have a car waiting for me. I will call y'all after I get home. Please do not blow up my phone. Kim, I will get my car tomorrow. I love y'all and thanks for everything," Lele said as they walked her to the door.

Lele walked out of the door and there was a pearl Cadillac outside and a chauffeur standing at the door waiting on her. She was so excited she didn't know what to do with herself. The chauffeur spoke in such a proper tone and looked as if he could be related to Darryl. They proceeded down the street, heading downtown. She wondered where they were going for a night of dancing. As they were driving, she glanced into the sky. There was a full moon out that night and the sky was decorated with the most beautiful stars. For a moment, she thought she saw the big dipper. When they arrived downtown, the streets were flooded with people. There were people everywhere. "I hope I didn't get all dolled up to walk the streets. The annual Greek and jazz festival started yesterday. People from all over the world come here for the festival. President Usiah even came last year," she thought to herself. The car began to slow down and Lele looked around, trying to figure out where they were going. The driver turned into the parking garage of the Stokes Tower. The Stokes Tower was in the heart of downtown and was the tallest building in the state. Only the most elite patronized that place. She wondered if they were going to the restaurant that's on the top of the tower. Lele couldn't wait to tell the girls about that one. Lele and the girls had driven there one day just to look inside the restaurant and to get a menu. As the driver approached the level for the restaurant, Lele looked in the mirror to check her hair and makeup. To her surprise, they bypassed the restaurant. She got a bit nervous. She thought that maybe she was in a runaway Cadillac because there was nothing else in the building past the restaurant. She asked the driver if they were close to their destination and he looked in the rearview mirror and just nodded his head.

"Oh, my God! We are on the roof of the Stokes Tower. The view is so beautiful from up here," she thought. She saw Darryl leaning against the rail, smiling with those perfect white teeth. He came towards the car. The chauffeur got out to open her door when Darryl signaled to him, he had it. "Darryl is so handsome. He has on a black suit, an electric blue shirt, and a nice silk tie. His goatee is trimmed, and he has a fresh haircut. There is a table set for two with a bottle of wine chilling. This man even has a band set up over in the corner. Lord, there he is," she said to herself.

"Hello, Alecia. You look darling this evening. I hope your ride here was a pleasant one," Darryl said.

"Hello, Mr. full of surprises. Yes, my ride was very pleasant. You don't look half bad yourself," she laughed.

"Alecia, may I have this dance?"

"You most certainly can," she smiled.

Darryl took her purse and placed it on the table. The band began to play *If this world were mine.* He took Alecia by the hand and pulled her in close to him. Alecia laid her head on his chest and he smelled so nice. "This just feels so right," Alecia said to herself. Alecia began to say something since she hadn't talked to him all day, when Darryl just told her to listen to the song and relax. So, she closed her eyes and listened to the words to the song.

By the end of the song, she was almost asleep. "It just feels like I belong with him. I could definitely see myself falling asleep on his chest for the rest of my life," she thought.

The band lowered the music, and Darryl took her by the hand again.

"Come on and have a seat, Alecia. Tonight, I want to treat you like the queen that you are. And if you will let me, I would love to continue that treatment for the rest of our lives," Darryl said, coming on strong.

"Darryl, I must admit, from the surprise at the salon, until now, you really have made me feel special. I have never felt like this before," she said, and then the waiter came to the table to pour some wine.

"I cannot believe I am on top of the Stokes Tower, having dinner. From up here, I can see the city lights for miles. There is a nice breeze too. Darryl has dinner prepared and a wait staff to serve our every need. It's as if we are in our own little private world," she pondered.

"Before we go on with our conversation, what are we eating tonight?" she asked. "I hope he doesn't think I am starving, but I am," she thought.

"I see you are hungry, huh? I hope you have had something to eat since breakfast," Darryl said, laughing. "I'm just kidding, sweetheart. I know how you said you love seafood, so that's what we are having. For starters, we have lobster bisque and a crab salad. For our entrée, we have Cajun chicken and shrimp pasta with garlic muffins and raspberry lemonade. If you aren't too stuffed after all of that, we have caramel brownie delights topped with ice cream and brandy butter sauce on a hot skillet," Darryl explained.

"Wow, Darryl, you really know how to make a girl feel special. I don't think I have ever felt this special before. Even if this relationship doesn't go anywhere, I want you to know that I feel like I have found a true friend in you. Well, I take that back," she said and laughed. "Bighead, why didn't you tell me you had a twin brother? You had me looking dumbfounded this morning."

Darryl laughed and said, "Well, Alecia, you didn't ask. I wish I could have been there to see your face. Derrell said it was quite hilarious, to say the least."

"Yeah, I guess it was funny. What other secrets do you have that I wouldn't ask about right off the top? I have told you just about everything about me. Anything else you want to know, you will have to stick around and spend some time with me to find out," she said. Alecia was trying to see if Darryl really had any long-term plans to get to know her or if he was just blowing hot air. She was not very blunt so that's the only way she could ask him. Alecia didn't want him to know that she was so into him the way that she was.

"I don't have any secrets, Alecia. I am just a country boy that loves God, work hard, and looking for my lost rib. What do you mean I have to stick around to find out everything else about you? Are you trying to see if I have sticktuitiveness? Girl, I told you when I met you that you were the one for me. We don't have to get married tomorrow, but I need to know from you, what do you want from me? What are your intentions?" Darryl asked.

"Whoa! Darryl is serious, I see. What are my intentions? I am the one that is supposed to ask that darn question. He asked me out on a date. He is really up on his game," she thought.

"Darryl, I see you are a very direct person. My intentions are to continue to serve God and wait for Him to do what He promised. From what I have seen these past two days, you appear to be everything I have ever prayed about and more. But I have to be honest with you. It actually appears to be too good to be true. It is almost like a fairytale. I really cannot afford to be hurt again, but I don't want to shut the door on you, and you could be my husband. I actually feel weird saying this to you only on the second day I met you. I don't want to rush into anything, but let's work on our friendship and see what the Lord is going to do," Alecia said, finishing her salad.

"I definitely understand everything you are saying. I myself do not desire to be hurt. My heart is made of flesh, just like yours. I just want us to be open with each other, enjoy the time we have together. My mother and grandparents were killed in a tragic accident when we were only ten years old. My great aunt took us in, and she cared for us the best she could in her old age. She died when we were fifteen, and we chose to live in her house and take care of ourselves. So, in actuality, Derrell, his wife and kids are the only family I have. I get lonely at times, just like I am sure you do. I just want someone to spend my time with and if that time turns into a lifetime, I will be grateful for that too," Darryl said as a tear dropped down his smooth chocolate skin.

Alecia grabbed Darryl's hand and leaned in close to him. She gently kissed his cheek to stop the tears from flowing. She hoped he didn't take her kiss the wrong way, but her heart was hurting for him. He only wanted somebody to love him and needed some love in return. Alecia was definitely falling for him. She knew that if it was God's will, she could give him that love his heart desired.

"Darryl, I hear you. Let's just enjoy our dinner and see what happens. I think we should share a brownie, though, because I am stuffed. And you should be too as much as you have eaten," she giggled, trying to switch the mood. That's one thing Alecia's

Pastor always ensured that they received on Sunday mornings, a mixture of emotions. The sermons were so convicting, you'll be crying. In the midst, he'll throw a few jokes in there to get you to laugh and by the end of service, the band plays a song you will have in your heart to carry you through the week," she thought to herself drifting away. Alecia must have really left the building in her mind because Darryl began calling her name.

"Alecia, Alecia, hello! What in the heavens are you thinking about that has you smiling like that? It must be me," Darryl said confidently with a smile.

She laughed and said, "No, Darryl, I wasn't thinking about you that time. I was thinking about the goodness of Jesus and all he has done for me. Boy, He's so good, I can shout right now. My soul looks back and wonders how I made it over."

"Yeah, I know what you're talking about. I can definitely relate. This brownie is rather pleasing to the tongue, don't you think?" Darryl asked.

"To say the least," she replied.

"I never knew the city was so beautiful from up here at night. I've only come up here early in the morning right before the break of dawn," Darryl said and leaned back in his chair.

"Oh, really now. What are you doing up here at all, mister? I know you are not bringing me somewhere that you bring your other lady friends," she said, nudging his arm.

"Girl, you are hilarious. No, Alecia, it's nothing like that, trust me. This is my place of refuge outside of church; the place where I come to clear my mind, when the weights of life are hovering over my head. When I need some peace, I come here. Sometimes I come here just to talk to God. It's a calming spot for me. You are the only person that I have ever shared this place with. This rooftop is a very intimate and private place for me," Darryl explained.

"He really shut me up," she thought to herself. "I didn't actually think he brought other women up here, but I just wanted to hear him say it."

"Oh, Darryl, that is so sweet. You really seem like you are a pretty put-together guy," she laughed. Then continued, "I have really enjoyed myself tonight. Believe me when I say that I wish the night didn't have to end, but it does.

It's getting late, and I have to get up for church bright and early in the morning," she said.

"Ditto, Madam Alecia. I didn't realize how late it was. Time sure does fly when you're having fun. I especially enjoy your company, but I know your friends are up waiting on you."

"Yeah, most likely they all are sitting by the phone. I already told them that I wasn't coming back to Kim's house. I'm just going to drive my truck tomorrow because if I go pick up my car, we will be up ALL night. At least with the phone, I can hang up on them. I ought not call them and make them mad," she laughed hysterically.

"That would be kind of funny, though," Darryl replied. "But please don't because Kim would be upset with me, especially after everything she went through to set up our meeting," Darryl said with an uh oh look on his face.

Alecia dropped her mouth. She thought to herself that she knew he didn't just say what she thought he said. Alecia wondered what he meant by 'everything she went through to set up our meeting.'

"Uh, excuse me, Darryl. Please remove your hand off of your face. Now, what did you just say?" she asked very firmly.

"It wasn't important, Alecia. I think my mouth just ran away from me. The words came out so quickly; I didn't realize I said that. Well, come on and get in the car, beautiful," Darryl said with a smile.

"I'll be ready in a minute. Darryl, you mean to tell me that Kim arranged for you to come to her house while the girls were there last night?" she asked.

Darryl hesitated and said, "Yes, Alecia, I confess. She told me that you didn't entertain hookups, so that was the only way for us to conveniently meet. But that doesn't really matter now, though, right?"

"That little scandalous, girl. I can't believe her. No, it doesn't matter. So, you must be the guy she was telling me about yesterday, and I told her no. Was there anything really wrong with her computer?"

Darryl laughed and said, "Girl, no. She just needed a new ink cartridge."

"I'm shocked. It's not very often that someone pulls something over on me. You know I am a very clever woman. I am not going to mention it to her, either. I'm going to wait a very long time before I bust her out," she said and stepped away from the table.

After they both were in the car, the chauffeur closed the door and off they went. Darryl took Alecia's hand and leaned his head back against the seat. She closed her eyes and listened to the music as they traveled through the city. Alecia planned to tell the driver to drop Darryl off at home first so he wouldn't know where she lived. But after having such a glorious time, she didn't mind him knowing where she resided anymore. "This just feels so right in my Spirit. I must admit, though, it's kind of scary. I pray this is the man for me." She thought.

CHAPTER FOUR

Getting it Out

S hantel was really nervous about the counselor coming that day. She hoped he didn't try to hypnotize her or anything. She knew there was no telling what would come out. Shantel told her boss she would work from home so that way her paycheck wouldn't be short. Gerome took the day off with pay, which was a blessing. She was grateful that Gerome had good benefits at the bus yard, because the pay wasn't hitting on anything. Dr. Roberts should be arriving at their home shortly.

"Hey, Shantel, sweetie. I dropped the kids off at the bus stop and made sure they got on the bus alright. Are you ready?" Gerome asked.

"Yes, I'm as ready as I can be," Shantel said. Then continued, "But I am a bit nervous, though. I wish I knew what questions he was going to ask."

"Aww, baby. It's good we don't know what questions he is going to ask. If we did, we would have rehearsed our answers, and that defeats the purpose. We need what's really going on in the inside to come out."

"Yea, I guess you're right," Shantel agreed.

"Hey, let's make a pact. No matter what comes out in these counseling sessions, we will not get angry at one another. No matter how bad it is or how shocked one of us may be. We both have to get to the point where we can express ourselves without there being an argument. Okay?" Gerome stated.

Before the two of them could shake on it, they heard the door chimes ringing. Shantel's face immediately turned red and her stomach balled up in knots. Gerome answered the door. In walked a man dressed in a nice linen suit. He was about five two and had a pair of specks hanging on his nose. He made you think of the nerd in your biology class.

"Hello, Mrs. Scott. I'm Dr. TL Roberts. It's nice to meet you and thank you for inviting me into your lovely home."

"Hello, Dr. You can just call me Shantel. Mrs. Scott sounds so formal. Welcome to our home. Please have a seat. Would you like something to drink before we get started?"

"No, thank you. I have a full schedule today, so we should just jump right on in," Dr. Roberts explained. "Shantel, we will begin with you for this first session. Let me just start my recorder here. Now, can you tell me a little about your childhood and your relationships with your mother and father?"

"Doc, I don't even know where to start. My whole life and my family are a life of dysfunction. I am the only girl of three children. My momma was an alcoholic, drug addict, and she never knew who my daddy was. She was high most of the time, so she slept with anybody that would give her a fix. She was very abusive and mean toward us when she was drunk. On her sober days, Momma was the sweetest woman you would ever want to meet. Momma would even take us to the park and for ice cream. Of course, those times were few and far between. We couldn't have friends over because Momma was drunk all of the time," Shantel wept.

"How did that make you feel as a child?"

"How did I know that question was coming up next? Here we go. My heart is racing, and my mind is in so many places right now. Should I open up to this total stranger? Hell, I don't know what to do." Gerome reached over and grabbed Shantel's hand to comfort her she guessed. "It definitely isn't working," Shantel said to herself.

"How did that make you feel as a child, Shantel?" Dr. Roberts asked again.

Shantel lifted her head and tried to regain her composure. "Well, doctor, that made me feel like the scum of the earth. It made me feel as if I should have never been born. There were so many days that I wished I was dead. I truly believed that death had to have been better than living like that. If there was a God, then He just didn't love me, either. All of my friends had loving parents that came to school functions and sat down together as a family for dinner. I used to cry almost every night because I felt so alone.

My two brothers ended up moving out once we got a little older because their grandparents came to their rescue. I had nobody to rescue me."

"Go on, Shantel," said Dr. Roberts.

"I can't do this," she screamed and cried. Shantel got up from the couch and ran to the bathroom. At that moment, she couldn't even explain the way she felt right then. Shantel knew she definitely couldn't go on, but she didn't want to let Gerome and the kids down. She was sitting on the toilet crying when she heard a knock on the door.

"Shantel, baby, it's me. Are you alright?" he asked but to no avail. "Baby, open the door and let me in. I am here for you. Come on, open the door."

Shantel wiped the tears from her face and opened the door. As soon as Gerome stepped in, she threw her head into his chest. He took his arms and squeezed her tight and told her to let it all out. Although the counseling was very hard for her, she appreciated the support he was giving her. She had never felt so close to him until that moment.

"Hey, you're doing great out there. Are you alright?"

"Gerome, this is too hard. My mind is going back to all of the terrible things I endured living with my mom, things that I had totally pushed out of my memory. I don't know if I can handle talking about them. I just don't know if I can continue."

"Shantel, I am not going to push you to do anything you are not comfortable with right now. Baby now is the time to get it all out, though. We have somebody here to help us through the pain of those memories. You are not alone, okay. I wish you would continue this session, but I will support whatever decision you make," Gerome said.

Shantel wiped her tears once again and said, "Thanks, Gerome. If I continue, promise me that you won't stop loving me, promise me that. I don't think I would be able to continue life knowing that you didn't love me anymore. There are just so many things that happened to me that you don't know about. I have been living with these horrific secrets, trying to deal with them alone. I can't see pass them, Gerome. They haunt me when I'm sleep, and they torture me when I'm awake."

"I promise, baby. When I vowed for better or worse, I meant it. All of those things are in the past anyway. We will just have to deal with them together and build from that. Come on, the doctor is waiting on us."

Gerome placed his arm around Shantel's neck, and they headed back to the living room. She had never finished any task she had ever started anyway. So, she decided to finish with the counseling session.

"Shantel, do you wish to continue?" Dr. Roberts asked.

"I want to, doc, but I really don't know if I can face these memories. I don't know, but I am willing to try."

"Your reactions are very normal. It can be a bit overwhelming at first once memories start running through your mind back and forth and you feel forced to face them. I promise, once you begin to talk about them and time passes, it will get easier. If you need to cry, scream, or run, please feel free to do it. Whatever way you have to express yourself to get it all out, you do it. We will continue with your relationship with your mother for this session and pick up

83

somewhere else next week. I believe the key to your marriage is the healing you need regarding your mother. So, tell me more about your relationship."

"Well, Dr., there is so much to share about her. One thing I can tell you is that I hate her very being. If she died today in that nursing home, I would not even go to her funeral. My momma did more than just beat me when she was drunk, but it was even worse when she was with her boyfriend getting high." As Shantel continued, the tension built. She hesitated. "You see, my momma used to make me have sex with my brother because she and her boyfriend got off on that. They just sat and watched. My brother would keep his eyes closed until the timer went off for us to stop because he couldn't stand the terror in my eyes," Shantel cried and immediately looked at Gerome.

Gerome dropped his head because he didn't want her to see his facial expression. He knew that would make her feel worse than she already did. He had to admit, though, that was very shocking.

"Gerome, how do you feel hearing that your wife served as a part-time hooker for her mother?" Dr. Roberts asked.

Gerome knew he had to be very careful of how he answered that question. His response would dictate Shantel's reaction during the counseling sessions.

"Well, Doc, I am extremely shocked that Shantel would keep something like that from me, but as I explained to her earlier, her past is the past. God allowed those things to happen to her for a reason, so I can't do anything but support her right now," Gerome said.

"I must say, Gerome, that is the honorable thing to do. I have had some cases where the spouses just flipped out once a secret had been revealed in a session. Then there are some that pretend that they are okay with the information and then treat their spouse differently once they get back home. So, Gerome, if there is something you want to say or ask, then now is the time to do it."

"No, Doctor, I am actually okay. I often wondered if Shantel had been raped or something because of how she responded to me sexually. So, this information is good to know." Gerome turned to Shantel and said, "Baby, for a while now, I thought that I just couldn't please you."

Shantel winked at Gerome and said, "I'm satisfied with only a touch from you."

"Alright, you two. Let's save some of that for later," Dr. Roberts laughed. "Gerome when a woman is raped, sometimes she feels as if it is her own fault. It also causes her to feel insecure and lowers her self-esteem. Often times, it plays a major role with women regarding trusting a man and having sexual intercourse. We will discuss those bedroom issues at a later session, though." Doctor Roberts knew that was the perfect time to offer some type of information regarding abused women.

"Shantel, hearing that from Gerome, does that make you feel more secure in yourself and marriage?" Dr. Roberts asked.

"Well, Doc, it's a start. As long as I have Gerome standing with me, then I know I can make it," expressed Shantel.

Before Doctor Roberts could ask his next question, his timer in his briefcase went off. Shantel put her hands to her face and started screaming.

"Shantel, baby. Baby. It's okay," Gerome assured her.

"I am sorry about my timer. I always set a timer before a counseling session to make sure we don't run over. It didn't register to stop it after Shantel mentioned her timer memories."

Gerome calmed Shantel down. He knew that was a bad moment for her.

"Again, Shantel, I apologize," Doctor Roberts said.

"Okay, that is all of the time we have for today. Until our next meeting, I want you to keep a journal. Think of any other happy times that you had with your mom. At our next meeting, we will discuss those times. Gerome, we will also bring you into the picture and discuss those bedroom issues. Thank you all again for inviting me into your home."

After Dr. Roberts left their home, Gerome sat next to Shantel. The mood in the house was so uneasy. He didn't know exactly what to say, so he said nothing.

He pulled the throw from the back of the couch and laid Shantel on his lap. They still had a while before the kids would arrive from school, so they just sat there quietly.

CHAPTER FIVE

Celebration Time

A few months later, the girls were having a gathering at Lele's house. All of the girls were there except Monay. They were having a special celebration for Monay since she was recently promoted to Captain on her military base. It would be easy to surprise her because she was always late for everything.

"Lele, did you remember to pick up the ice cream from Wally-World?" Kim asked.

"Girl, I decided not to get any ice cream. I just purchased an ice cream cake instead. That was the cheapest way to go."

"Lele, you are so frugal, girl. I don't think it would have been that much with the three of us splitting the costs. For you to have so much money, you surely don't like to spend any of it.

We keep telling you, you cannot take that money with you," Shantel laughed.

"Girl, forget both of y'all. I just like to utilize wisdom when it comes to spending. Anyway, I am paying for your dresses for my wedding," Lele said.

"Uh, wedding? Lele, did we miss something? You and Darryl have only been going out a few months and you are talking about a wedding already," Kim inquired.

"Kim, I know. What happened to the Lele we knew," Shantel laughed.

"You all need to stop being funny. I have always told y'all I wanted to get married again. Kim, call Monay and see where she is," Lele switched subjects.

Before Kim could finish dialing the numbers, the doorbell rang. They figured that Monay had arrived. Shantel opened the door and Monay was standing there with a bottle of beer in her hand. Monay knew that Lele didn't allow drinking in her house, so she sat the bottle outside. She would pick it up when she got ready to leave.

"Hey, Shantel! Girl, am I late?" Monay asked.

"Aren't you always late? Get your trifling butt on in here so we can eat. We have been waiting on you," Shantel said.

When Monay walked into the family room, she saw lots of balloons and streamers. On the back wall, she saw a banner that read, "Congratulations Monay." Then all of the girls screamed, "Surprise!"

Monay stood there with a big smile on her face. "Y'all did all of this for me?" she asked. "I can't believe y'all would do this for me."

"Monay, you know you are our girl. You are a single, black female and you are in charge of your entire brigade. That is something to be proud of, especially since you didn't sleep your way to the top. We hope not anyway. We couldn't let this moment pass us by," Lele laughed.

"Group hug everybody," Monay said.

All of the girls embraced each other with so much love. They knew that their friendships were rare, so they truly cherished every moment they spent together.

"Now, can we eat? Lele, did you make me some of your famous rotel?" Monay asked.

"Girl, now you know there is no party without rotel. I made extra because I knew you would want to take some home," Lele said.

Everyone was fixing their plates when Lele asked, "Kim are you okay? You are not really acting yourself tonight. What's going on with you, girl?

"Nothing much. I have just been a little tired lately. I need to get some rest this weekend. My students have been really acting out this week," replied Kim.

"Kim, you know you can't lie well. What's up for real? You seem kind of distant. It's us, your girls. Spit it out," Shantel said.

"Now if it's something that's gross, keep it to yourself until we finish eating," Lele laughed.

"Honestly, I'm okay."

"Alright, we are not going to beg you to tell us. Shantel, what's going on in your world? Are you and Gerome still going to counseling?" Monay asked.

"Yes, we are only going every two weeks now. The counselor said that since I am showing so much progress, we don't have to attend every week."

"That's good, Shantel. I am so proud of y'all because, girl, you were scaring us for a minute. We didn't know if y'all were going to make it or not," Lele said.

"Well, everything still is not perfect. We have a long way to go, but at least we are on the right track. We are striving for a spiritually healthy marriage. Lele, you shut up anyway. Just because you are all in love now, let's not get carried away," Shantel smirked.

"Yeah,, Lele, what's up with y'all these days. We don't even hear from you as much anymore," Monay said.

"Well, girls, you know how it is when you're in love," Lele laughed.

"In love?! What? You have got to be kidding me. Girl, have you given up the booty yet? If you haven't, then there is no way for you to be in love, chick," Monay said.

"Monay, girl, please. I am not THAT in love. Nobody drops their panties like you. Darryl and I are just taking everything one day at a time. We will probably get married in a couple of years or so.

I am not trying to rush into anything. I have already had one failed marriage and that's enough. But I can tell you one thing, nobody has ever treated me the way he does. He calls me every morning and every night for devotion. You can't ask for more than that. Everything is not all about sex. You need to make sure that man can pray you through when you are going through," Lele said.

"Well, miss goodie two shoes, when are you going to allow him to meet AD?" Monay asked.

Everyone knew that Lele was very overprotective of AD. However, none of them could understand why. That's a part of her life she did not openly discuss with anybody.

"I don't know exactly when, but it will probably be soon. I really want them to have a good relationship before I could seriously think about marrying Darryl. AD will be home next week for a break. So, we will see what happens."

"Yeah, whatever, Lele. You just want everything to be so perfect. You get on my nerves with that mess." Monay turns to Kim, "Kim, what in the hell is wrong with you?

There has to be something because you usually come to your little friend's rescue. You hadn't opened your damn mouth, not one time," Monay asked.

"It's nothing that I want to talk about right now. Can y'all just respect that?" Kim said.

"Nope, hell no. You always want to know everybody else's business but want to keep yours to yourself. So, tell us what's up," Monay said.

"Kim, do I need to get the oil? Girl, now you know we can pray about whatever it is that has your heart heavy," Lele questioned.

"Prayer would be good right now," Kim said.

"Lord, PLEASE no prayer while I'm trying to eat. Y'all know Lele pray too darn long," Shantel laughed.

Lele moved so she could sit by Kim.

"Kim, boo, what's bothering you, girl?" Lele asked.

Kim looked at her and the water welled up in her eyes. Kim was very hesitant about telling them what was wrong, but she knew they would not leave her alone. So, she figured she should just go ahead and tell them.

Kim sat up straight and said, "My cycle is two weeks late. I'm so afraid to take a pregnancy test because I just don't want to face another disappointment. It seems like me and James have been trying our entire marriage to conceive and nothing happens. We sit in church and watch all of the little teenage girls have babies back to back and nothing for us and we are living in His will. James prays so fervently. He told me one day that he wondered if we would ever have a baby of our own. I so desperately want to give him what he desires. There is not a worse feeling as a wife, than not to be able to give your husband something that your body was created to produce. I have read so many places of how people get pregnant with fibroids. I just hope I can."

"Aww, Kim, girl. You know God has everything under control. How about if you take a test with all of us with you," Lele said.

"Lele, where are we going to get a test from? Your stuff has cobwebs on it, so I know you don't have any in the medicine cabinet," Shantel laughed.

"Girl, now you know Monay keeps a test in her bag," said Lele.

"You got that right. Ept is always needed in case of emergencies," Monay said.

"Thanks, y'all, but I don't know. I just don't know if I am ready for another disappointment. I haven't said anything to James about it. I am so tired of getting his hopes up high, only for another letdown. He's always very understanding and tries so hard to comfort me and he needs comforting himself. I just feel so guilty. Sometimes I feel less than a woman. It's all my fault," Kim cried.

"Kim, I wish you would stop saying that. It is not your fault. How can it be your fault because you have fibroids? God just has his own perfect timing. Stop beating yourself up about your rape and having fibroids. You can always adopt, girl," Monay said. "People adopt all of the time. If you buy you a newborn baby, it can be just like it yours."

Kim cried even harder after Monay said that. She thought, why did she have to adopt a baby when she was perfectly healthy. She also remembered that James told her recently that if she didn't get pregnant within a year, then they would adopt. Kim cried even more because in her heart, she felt she couldn't get pregnant because of her hidden secret.

"Monay, shut your big mouth and give us the darn test. You only make things worse," Lele shouted.

"Okay, okay. You already know I'm sorry, Kim. I was just trying to offer other options. Some people on this earth won't bear children, but that doesn't stop them from being a mother. That's all I'm saying," Monay explained.

"And all we are saying is that nothing is impossible for God. When will you learn that when people are going through, they don't need to hear the negativity and doubt," Shantel said.

"Whatever, here you go, Kim. Do you want me to go in there with you?" Monay asked.

"Uh, no! Monay she is not a child. Besides, if she needed someone to go with her, you would not be the one to be with her. I think Lele should go," Shantel said.

"No, I can go alone. Thanks for the offer, though. I will be back in a moment. Hopefully, with good news," Kim smiled.

Kim walked down the hall and went into the bathroom and Lele began fussing. "Monay, you need to just shut up sometime. When Kim comes back out, don't you open your big mouth. How long does it take to get the pregnancy test results?"

"It only takes one minute," Monay replied. "After that, you will see a pink line or a pink cross."

Five minutes had passed, and the girls got a bit anxious. Suddenly, they heard a loud scream. Lele, Monay, and Shantel took off running down the hall. They all thought that maybe Kim had seen the pink cross. By the time they arrived at the door, they heard Kim crying and asking God 'why.'

"Kim, sweetie, open the door. Let us come in," Lele said.

"Come on, Kim, open up," pleaded Shantel.
Kim would not open the door. She just continued to cry and scream. The girls figured then that it had to have shown a negative sign. The three continued to knock and ask Kim to open up, but she wouldn't. The only thing she would say is that she wanted to die and that she could not go home like that.

After she said that, Shantel had a great idea. It had been a while since they all had a slumber party, so she called Gerome and told him they were going to turn the celebration into a slumber party. Gerome didn't mind at all, but he knew that something must have been wrong since Shantel called so late, though.

"Y'all, what are we going to tell James? Kim won't even come out of the bathroom, so I know she is not going to call. If she did call, he would immediately know something was wrong with her," Lele said.

"I say call and tell him that she got drunk and can't drive home," Monay said.

"That might work. He will probably think it's a little strange since Kim doesn't really drink and Lele don't allow drinking in her house. But hey, it's worth a try. We can tell him that Kim picked up Monay's cup by mistake and that's how she got drunk," Shantel said.

"Okay, Monay you call James," Lele laughed. "You know I am not about to tell that lie.

While Monay called James, Kim and Lele went back to the bathroom's door, but Kim still would not open the door. They sat at the bathroom door for at least an hour until Kim finally came out. The girls all cuddled up together on the sofa, telling jokes trying to make Kim feel better.

KIA STOKES

CHAPTER SIX

Coming Together

A D, I am so glad that you are home for a couple of weeks. I have missed you so much," Alecia said, sitting at their breakfast table.

Alecia was planning on telling AD about her relationship with Darryl, but she was a bit unsure of how he would react. She definitely didn't want him to react negatively because she really did care about Darryl, but she would not jeopardize her relationship with AD. Alecia still felt really guilty at times because of what happened to him.

"I know, Mom. It will be summer soon, and I am looking forward to it. Where are we going for summer vacation?" AD asked.

"Sweetheart, I don't know where we are going yet. I haven't even really thought about it. Do you have anywhere in mind? Where are some of your friends going for the summer?"

"Most of them are going to Disneyland in California. But I wish we could go to a beach somewhere. Disneyland brings back too many memories of when we used to go as a family. So, I really don't want to go there."

"I can understand that, son. Well, I'm sure if we put our heads together, we will come up with somewhere fun."

As they continued to talk over breakfast, Alecia's phone vibrated on the table. She glanced over at it, and it was Darryl. She decided not to answer the phone because she didn't want AD asking questions.

"Mom, aren't you going to get your phone? I thought you were on call today."

"That wasn't the hospital, it was a friend of mine."

"Was it Miss Kim or Miss Shantel? I hadn't seen them in a while," AD inquired.

"No, AD, that was another friend of mine calling that I want you to meet. He is anxious to meet you," Alecia said hesitantly.

"Mom, did you say he?" AD asked.

"Yes, AD, I said he. My friend's name is Darryl. We are only friends, but we do spend a lot of time together when you're at school. How do you feel about sharing me with another person?"

"Mom, exactly how close are y'all? Is he someone you just like to spend time with, or could this friendship move to another level?"

Alecia could not believe her ears. She always knew that AD was more mature than most children his age, but boarding school had really grown him up.

"My little boy is turning into a young man," Alecia thought to herself.

"Well, AD, to be honest with you, I really do care for him. I would like for us to take our relationship to another level, but I would love to have your blessing. I do not want to do anything that would jeopardize our relationship," explained Alecia.

"Well, Mom, I know I can't have you to myself forever…"

Before AD could finish his statement, Alecia interrupted him. "Baby, I know not forever, but if you need me to yourself until you are off to college, then I'm yours. I want you to know that you always come first in my life."

"I know that, Mom. So, when do I meet this fellow? He does understand that I won't be calling him daddy, right?"

"Yes, AD, he is very aware of that. I also told him that if you weren't okay with our relationship, then we would have to stop seeing each other. Do you want to meet him today or later on in the week? He invited the two of us out to his family's ranch today. He thought maybe that you would like to ride the horses."

"Horses? We haven't ridden horses in years. I would love to go and do that. That is going to be so much fun."

"I am very happy to hear you say that AD. I will call him back and let him know. He is repairing someone's computer right around the corner; so, it won't take him long to get here. Why don't you go upstairs and put your clothes on," Alecia said.

Alecia was so excited. That was the first guy she had ever even considered introducing to AD. She hoped that he was the one for her. Alecia didn't believe in introducing her son to every man she met. She knew that if the relationship didn't work out, then AD would be left with mixed emotions. Most children in similar situations call some man daddy they wouldn't ever see again. So, Alecia knew that was something that she would never do unless she was extremely confident about what God had spoken to her.

Alecia called Darryl and shared the good news with him. He told her he had just finished the computer and he would be there in a couple of minutes.

****

A few minutes later, Alecia heard Darryl pulling up outside. She hurried to the door to meet him. Before he could enter the door good, she gave him a big hug and kiss on the nose.

"Hey, Alecia. Did you miss me that much? I have never been greeted with a holy hug and a kiss from you," he laughed. "Have you gotten a Word from the Lord or what?"

"Darryl, stop. I am just so happy that AD wants to meet you. He even told me that he knew he couldn't have me for the rest of his life. He is actually looking forward to meeting you. You know how hard we have been praying for you and AD to have a good relationship," explained Lele. "That is more important to me than anything."

"Cupcake, I told you not to be a worrywart. God assured me that everything would fall into place. As long as AD and me respect each other, we won't have any problems. I know he loves you and I do too. We both think you are special, so I know we will hit it off."

As Darryl was speaking, AD came downstairs. Alecia became even more nervous.

"AD, come here, baby. I want you to meet Darryl. Darryl, this is my son, Addonte'," Alecia said.

Darryl extended his hands towards AD and they shook.

"Hello, Addonte', I am very pleased to meet you. I wasn't sure if Alecia was ever going to allow us to meet."

"Hi, Mr. Darryl. I am glad to meet you, as well. So, you are my mom's hidden secret, I suppose," AD said sarcastically.

"AD, let's not be sarcastic now," Alecia interrupted.

"Oh, Alecia, he's alright," Darryl said and continued. "Addonte', you don't have to call me mister. I know that is the respectful thing to do, but it just sounds so formal. Why don't you just call me D or Big D? Will that work, man?" Darryl asked.

"Yes, that will work if it is okay with Mom. I don't want to go against anything that she has taught me," he looked at his mom.

"Yes, AD, that is fine with me. Is everyone ready to go? We have a thirty-minute drive ahead of us," Alecia stated.

"Let's go then. Addonte', you can ride on the front seat with me, so we can get to know each other. Your mom can just ride on the back and read a book or something," Darryl chuckled.

"Alright, Darryl. This will not turn into tag team against Mom day. I think I will take a nap. I am a little tired," Alecia laughed as they got into the jeep.

They stopped by the gas station to fill up and then embarked on their thirty-minute journey out to the country. AD and Darryl talked all of the way while Alecia slept. They knew Alecia was tired but didn't know how tired. She did a good job showing them just how tired because she snored the entire trip.

When they arrived at the ranch, the horses were saddled and ready. AD and his dad used to ride horses all of the time when they were on vacation. That was the last thing they did together before their little incident. Darryl had just purchased 4 new four-wheelers to keep at the ranch for family use. It was going to be a surprise for Alecia for their next trip to the ranch. When AD saw the four-wheelers sitting under the tree, his eyes lit up.

"Oh, Mr. Darryl, I mean Big D, are those four-wheelers? Can I ride one? I have been wanting a four-wheeler for so long," AD asked with excitement.

"AD, don't get all bent out of shape. I am sure you can ride one," Alecia interrupted.

"Addonte', you can do more than ride one. You can take ownership of one if you want. Transporting them back and forth would be a bit much, though, so you can keep it stored here at the ranch," Darryl said.

"Really Big D? I can have one? My very own four-wheeler," AD exclaimed. "Can we ride those first? Please, Big D. Let's ride them first and then ride the horses."

"Sure, Addonte.' Whatever you want to do is fine," Darryl said.

"I will be here under the tree until y'all finish playing with your toys," Alecia said.

"I don't think so, Cupcake. You will be riding with us. You are not getting off that easy."

"Darryl, seriously, I'm okay. You guys go on and have fun."

"Mom, can you please come with us? It will be so much fun. Please, Mom."

"Maybe the next time," Alecia said.

Out of nowhere, Darryl grabbed Alecia and picked her up. She started screaming at him to put her down. AD was sitting on his four-wheeler, laughing and yelling at Darryl to get her.

"Darryl, put me down, boy. I am not playing with you. Put me down. Those things are dangerous, and I might break a nail," Alecia laughed.

It seemed as though they were having so much fun as a family. Darryl carried Alecia over to the pink and green four-wheeler and put her on it. She tried to get off until Darryl whispered something in her ear.

"Okay, guys, I guess I will ride this thing with y'all once. What about my hair? Torri just relaxed my hair yesterday," Alecia argued.

"I'm sure if I call Torri, she will hook you back up," Darryl replied.

"Okay, how do you work this thing? Is it like driving a car?" Alecia inquired.

"Mom, you are hilarious. I will show you."

"Yeah, Addonte', get down and let's help your mother out."

The two talked Alecia through operating the four-wheeler and they were all on their way. They were having a wonderful time going back and forth from four-wheelers to horses. The three had only been out there for a couple of hours when clouds covered the sky. They weren't sure if it would rain or not. Rain wasn't in the forecast, but they could never tell in Georgia. So, they parked the four-wheelers in the garage and put the horses back in the stable.

"Instead of heading back, why don't we go up to the main house and fix something to eat. While we're doing that, AD, you can go to the game room and play, or watch movies in the theater," Darryl suggested.

"Big D, you all have a theater too?" he was amazed.

"Yes, we do. I will show you around when we get up the hill. We have a swimming pool, tennis court, and a lake with kayaks."

AD turned to his mom and said, "Mom, can we sell our house and move to the ranch?"

"I don't know about that, AD. I am sure you are welcome to come here whenever you're home from school. Right, Darryl?"

"Yes, Alecia, you are right."

Alecia still couldn't believe how well AD and Darryl were getting along together. Since he was the only man, she had introduced him to since his dad, she thought he would automatically reject him.

"I will start fixing us a snack while you two are on your tour," Alecia said.

AD and Darryl began their tour of the ranch, and Alecia looked for something to cook in the kitchen. She noticed a can of chopped chicken, so she decided to make some chicken salad sandwiches.

"I am so happy right now, I can eat a can of sardines and be satisfied," Alecia thought to herself.

It took a half-hour for Darryl and AD to finish touring the house. After that, the three sat down and had their first family dinner.

****

"So Kimmie, when are you going to tell me the truth about your girls' night? We have been together too long for you to think you can pull something over my head," James asked.

"James, do we have to continue to keep going around and around about this? Girls night is over, so can we please move on? We just decided to have a slumber party at the last minute," Kim said in a frustrated voice.

"No, Kim, we cannot move on. I am not going to keep asking you over and over because you are going to tell me. You are my wife, and I was nice enough to allow you to stay out all night with your friends; even though I knew Shantel called and told me a boldfaced lie. I have always been an understanding husband, but my patience is about to run out. So, if we are going to keep our communication open and you want to freely go where you want, then your lips better get to moving."

Tears rolled down Kim's face as always when James was stern with her. She did not want to tell him what was really going on. Sometimes when they talked about children, he would just shut down. At times, it was as hard for him as it was for her. Every time his countenance would change, Kim would only feel worse.

"Kimmie, you may as well start talking because the tear game is not going to work this time. You are always open when it comes to your girls' night. You usually come home and light my ear up. I have been waiting for weeks, and you haven't opened your mouth. Were you with another man or something?"

"James, would you just stop it? Just shut up?"

"Well, say something, damn it."

"Okay, okay. James, I have been trying to handle everything on my own. My cycle was late two weeks, and I thought I was pregnant. At Lele's house, I took a pregnancy test, and it was negative. I locked myself in the bathroom and wouldn't come out. That's why they had to come up with something to tell you because I didn't want you to know. We ended up praying and fell asleep on the couch," Kim cried.

"Kimmie, why wouldn't you want me to know? We are in this thing together. Why would you keep something like that from me?"

"James, I am so tired of disappointing you with negative pregnancy tests. I see the way you look at me when it is negative. I see the disappointment in your eyes, and that just pierces my heart. It is trying enough for me to deal with the disappointment myself, without adding yours to it."

"Kim, I guess I never realized that my body language was speaking so loudly. I have to be honest with you, though. To see you in all of this pain, really makes my heart hurt. I know you are not going to want to hear what I have to say, but I think you should go ahead and have those fibroids removed."

"What? You know the doctor said if I had that surgery, then they might have to perform a hysterectomy too."

"I'm tired of you always in constant pain and complaining about heavy cycles when you do have them. We are not going to worry about what the doctor said. Hopefully, it won't be as bad as they think once they start the operation. I have seen plenty of cases like that. Come here and sit down. Kim, I want you to have my child as much as you do, but baby, if we have to adopt a newborn, I will be okay with that. As long as I have you, I am satisfied. So what if we have to adopt, so be it."

Kim screamed to the top of her lungs. She refused to accept an adoption. She reflected on the abortion she had, the one that her husband or friends did not know about. She has always wanted to tell him, but she didn't want him to think she was the reason she couldn't get pregnant again. That little secret was eating her alive every day. Kim hadn't told a single soul about the abortion. She figured adopting wouldn't be that bad, if she hadn't had that abortion. Kim felt like God was punishing her. All of her friends thought she was raped by a stranger, but she was actually never raped at all. She had an abortion for a more selfish reason.

"Why is God punishing me this way," she yelled. "If I have to adopt, then I rather not have a child at all. I shouldn't have to settle for some unwanted child."

"Kim, that is your flesh talking right now. Just calm down and listen to what you are saying. We will have a child. Now what avenue we have to take, only the Lord knows. I know you are upset, but we will have children. So, you can get that out of your mind that we are not. Go ahead and make a doctor's appointment next week. I will call the television station to find out about some of the children they advertise on their show that needs a home. We can change someone else's life as well as our own lives, baby."

"Like I said, I am not adopting a baby. You go ahead and adopt one on your own. You will be raising that child alone," Kim declared.

James could not believe what he just heard. The woman he loved so dearly had just threatened to leave him. He knew that was not the woman he married saying something like that.

"Kimberly, what did you just say? Did you just threaten to leave me? I would advise you to stop allowing the devil to make you say stupid stuff. If you can't bear children, then we are adopting! I am the head of this house. You will not deprive me of being a father. I am not going to allow you to destroy my dreams," James explained.

After he finished stating his claim, Kim cried profusely. James attempted to comfort Kim, but she just shewed him away. When she got like that, she wouldn't deal with anyone, not even him. She usually did that for weeks at a time. He knew that Kim didn't mean to shut him out, so he was never offended. James went into the other room and secretly contacted the news station so he could get some information about adoption.

****

It's the end of the fiscal year for the military and it's time for Monay to take her yearly medical examination. The physician took her vital signs and most of her numbers were looking really good. Monay was pleased to know that because she had not been taking care of herself the way that she needed too. She was eating out at multiple restaurants every day and didn't know what the word exercise meant. Monay knew she had to pass her physical or the military would put her on a special eating plan. If the diet plan didn't work, then she would be discharged. The military was her livelihood, so she knew that couldn't happen. The military provided her with free travel and access to available men, single or married.

"I was a little nervous about my appointment today," Monay said to the doctor.

"Why is that, Ms. Myers? You have been seeing me for years, and everything has always worked out," replied the doctor.

"Well, Doc, I haven't been feeling my best. Lately, I haven't had any energy and been very weak. Sometimes I feel numbness throughout my body, and I can't seem to remember things at times. The other day I was driving, and my vision became blurry. I kind of feel like something is definitely not right in my body."

"That sounds interesting. After I finish with your physical, I will send a technician in to withdraw some blood. We should have those results back in a couple of days. I would like to see you again tomorrow to begin a series of tests because those symptoms sound pretty serious. In the meantime, you should take a few days off work and relax a little," explained the doctor.

The doctor knew those symptoms sounded like some he heard so many times before. He didn't want to alarm Monay of what he thought they meant.

"Doctor, what do you think all of these symptoms mean."

"Aww, Ms. Myers, we are not going to jump to any conclusions. Let's just wait and examine the results after all the necessary tests have been run. I'll see you later."

"Okay, doctor, if you say so," Monay said. After the doctor left the room, Monay sat there with a very uneasy feeling. She wanted to call her girls and ask for prayer, but she really didn't want to bother them if nothing was really wrong.

"Lord, I wish you would hear me," thought Monay. Monay hadn't been to church in years, so naturally, she had no relationship with God. She often joked that God wouldn't know her if they were sitting down having lunch together. Monay wasn't ready to be sold out for Jesus like Lele was, so she just stayed in her lane, which was led by the devil. She believed the bible when God said that you had to be either hot or cold because lukewarm would get you spewed out of His mouth. So, Monay decided not to even try to communicate with God because He wouldn't hear her.

****

It was less than a week when Monay received a call saying she needed to come into her doctor's office as soon as possible. That made her nervous because her appointment wasn't until a few days later. She had received results in the mail already from some of the tests that she had taken. All of those results came back negative. Monay took a leave from work until she knew what was going on. She had even taken a vacation from the club. Monay hadn't been out in days, nor had she talked to her girls. All of them had been calling, but she just sent the calls to voicemail.

Monay got dressed and headed out. The doctor's office was only five minutes from her house. As Monay sat behind the wheel, her mind wondered. She wondered what was so important that she needed to come in so quickly. Monay thought that maybe she had HIV or something, and that was God's way of punishing her for being a slut.

After minutes of driving, she arrived at the office. When she walked in, they called her straight back. That was something that never happened, so she knew something was really wrong. She was sitting on the table with her entire body trembling when the doctor walked in.

"How are you doing, Ms. Myers," the doctor asked.

"Not too well at all. I am a nervous wreck about being called in today."

"I can understand that. Have you been experiencing any of the symptoms that you complained about at your previous visit?"

"Yeah, I have. On some days I feel great, and then on others, I can barely move because I am so weak. What does all of this mean?" she inquired.

"Well, I don't have good news. After extensive tests, the findings are startling. The results show that you are suffering from the beginning stages of multiple sclerosis."

Before the doctor could finish, Monay sounded off with a horrible cry. She didn't know a lot about multiple sclerosis other than what she saw on television shows. However, she did know that it was a debilitating disease.

"Oh, my God! How did this happen to me? Am I going to die? Am I going to end up in a wheelchair or bedridden? Oh, Lord, help me," she cried.

"Please try to calm down, Ms. Myers."

"Calm down? This is my damn life, Doctor. How in the hell am I going to be able to go and party with my friends? How am I supposed to work? I just received a promotion on my job. They are going to kick me out of the military when they receive this report."

"Please, just listen. MS is a disease of the immune system that attacks the central nervous system. Disease onset usually occurs in young adults, and it is more common in women. There is no cure for MS, but it can be treated to prevent new attacks and prevent disability. There are many people that live full, healthy lives without becoming bedridden and losing all mobility. It is going to be up to you to educate yourself on this disease. We have referred you to a MS specialist, made you an appointment, and will get you started on treatments as early as tomorrow."

Monay just sat on the table and cried uncontrollably. She could not believe that something like that could be happening to her.

"I recommend that you remain on leave until you have had extensive treatments for your condition. I hate to do this, but I am going to have to forward my findings to your medical file. This will read as a failure for your physical examination," the doctor continued reluctantly.

"My life is over. I am such a failure," cried Monay. "What kind of love is this from God? They told me God was a loving God, but he is definitely being cruel to me."

"Oh, Ms. Myers, you are a fighter. You can beat this disease with a strong support system. I urge you to call your family and friends so they can help you through this. I am not going to lie to you and tell you as if it's going to be easy, because it is not. However, you can make it through. If you think you are defeated in your mind, then you are already defeated. As a man thinketh, so is he," the doctor said as he exited the room.

As Monay sat all alone and wept, her mind wondered. Pictures she had seen on television begin to flash across her mind. Pictures of herself in a wheelchair, getting around on a walker, and needing 24-hour assistance in her home, rolled across her mind so clear as if she was seeing a motion picture. Her tears were flowing so steadily, she couldn't even stop them. A nurse walked in to check on her, but she couldn't get through to her. She offered to call someone for her, but Monay declined the offer and asked her to leave.

Monay knew she needed someone to drive her home because she was hysterical, but who? Lele, Kim, or Shantel? "I guess I should call Lele since she is the most comforting, plus she won't mention any of this to the other girls until I am ready." Monay scuffled to find her cell phone to call Lele.

"Hey, Lele, girl, are you busy?"

"Monay, is that you? You don't sound like yourself. What's up?"

"I need you to come and pick me up."

"Girl, me and Darryl are watching wedding videos. What man's wife has caught you with her husband, and he left you on the curb?" Lele laughed.

"Never mind!" she slammed the phone in her ear.

That wasn't like Monay not to be able to take a joke, so Lele knew something had to be wrong.
She called Monay back, but she didn't answer. She kept calling until finally, she answered.

"Hey, Monay, girl, I'm sorry. What's wrong? Tell me where you are, and I am on the way."

"I am at RKS Family Clinic on Terry Rd. I need you to come and pick me up. Please," Monay cried.

"Okay, I'm leaving right now."

Lele automatically started praying for Monay because she could hear the rattle in her voice over the phone.

It took Lele fifteen minutes to get to the doctor's office. When she pulled up, Monay was sitting outside on the hood of her car. Lele jumped out and ran over to her. She was anxious to know what the problem was.

"Hey, Monay, girl, what's going on?" she asked embracing her.

"Hey, can you drop me off at home? I will come back another day and pick up my car," asked Monay.

"Sure, girl, come on and get in. What is wrong?" Lele inquired.

Lele and Monay got in the car and headed down the highway.

"So Monay, are you going to tell me what's wrong?"

"Lele, I just received a really bad doctor's report. A report that will change my life forever," she said in a somber tone.

"What is it, Monay? You are acting like you are about to die. Girl, you sound like you have HIV or something?"

"Lele right now is not the time for your little smart jokes. No, I don't have HIV. Do you think I should because I sleep around?"

"Hey, I didn't mean it like that. I don't mean to fight with you while you are in this state. I'm sorry, Monay. Tell me, what did the doctor say?"

"The doctor has diagnosed me with multiple sclerosis. I'm going to end up cripple."

"Oh, my God, Monay! Multiple sclerosis? I am so sorry."

"Yea, me too."

"When will you start treatments?" Lele asked.

"Tomorrow I go to see a specialist and treatments begin then. The specialist is at the hospital where you work. Will you be working tomorrow?"

"Yes, I will be there. It has to be pretty serious for you to start treatments tomorrow. What time is your appointment?"

"My appointment is at 9:15 in the morning, but I have to be there at 8:30 to complete all of the necessary paperwork," answered Monay.

"Okay. I will just call and let the hospital know that I won't be on duty until after lunch. That way I will have time to take you to your appointment and take you back home."

"Thank you so much, Lele. Please don't tell Shantel and Kim yet. I am really trying to cope with this myself before I tell them."

"Girl, you know my mouth is sealed. But you know how they are when they feel like they are being left out. They don't like us to have secrets, so you might not want to keep it from them too long."

"I'm sure they would understand. They have enough going on in their own lives anyway.
Why should I burden them with my problems? One reason I called you is that you aren't going through anything. You are on the lovers highway with not a care in the world."

"Girl, what you are going through is not a burden on anybody. That's what friends are for. We are here to help each other through when we are at our lowest points in life. And Monay, don't think that I am not going through anything just because I am not going through the same things you are. We all have different tests and trials."

"Yea, I know, Lele. Thanks for taking time away from your honey to come and get me."

As they pulled up to Monay's house, Lele had a great idea. "Monay, how about you pack an overnight bag and we have a slumber party like the old days? I will call Darryl and let him know because he was supposed to be coming back to the house."

"Girl, no. You don't have to change your plans for me. I will be alright."

"Monay, go in the house and pack a bag. You are my girl, and you should not be alone tonight.
I will be in the car until you get back. I am going to call Darryl."

"Okay, Lele, whatever you think is best," Monay said and closed the door. Then she turned around and said, "Thanks for being my friend."

CHAPTER SEVEN

Need Some Loving

"Hey, Gerome, baby, get the door. That should be Dr. Rob," yelled Shantel from the other room.

"I'm on the toilet. Can you get it?"

Shantel laughed and said, "Boy, you are a mess. I will get it."

Dr. Roberts walked in and gave Shantel a very warm hug. "Hello, Shantel, how is your day going?"

"Today is a good day. Gerome will be out in a minute."

"Okay. Well, I will just take my usual seat and get my recorder ready. This will be a short session today. Shantel, I do want to tell you that you have made tremendous progress over these past weeks and months.

I have noticed the change in you and it appears that you and Gerome's relationship has improved as well."

"I agree, Doctor," Gerome walked in and interrupted. "Shantel has been like a new woman around here. We could still use a little help in the bedroom, though."

Shantel shot him a look of disbelief.

"Well, that's what we will be discussing today. Gerome, we will begin with you. Tell me about your sex life," Dr. Rob stated.

"Well, we really don't have one. Most times, we make love if it is a holiday or a special occasion. Even at those times, it might be only one round. Just when the getting gets good, Shantel is through. Now when we were just dating, I couldn't keep her off me. We would have good wild sex wherever and whenever we had the opportunity. Sometimes in a hotel, the car, in the park, wherever. As soon as we got married, it seems like we started practicing abstinence. Even now, when we make love, it seems as if she is doing it out of obligation. I don't think she enjoys it at all."

Shantel sat there with a look of disbelief on her face. She probably didn't imagine that Gerome would just put it all out there like that. But she knew that changes could not be made without being open and telling the truth.

"Gerome, please continue."

"When we first married and I touched her, she would jump out of her sleep, terrified. Then there were times that she would have a nightmare. Looking in hindsight now, I understand. Clearly then I was lost. But we prayed about the nightmares, and eventually, she stopped having them. But that still hasn't improved our sex life. I joke with Shantel and tell her that when we do have sex, she gets pregnant," Gerome laughed.

"Gerome, when a woman has been traumatized sexually in any form and the issue not treated, it tends to turn them off about sex. A woman walks around with all of that hurt inside and sex is the last way to express how they feel. One client told me that to have sex was not showing her true love. I don't agree with that comment, however, there are a lot of wounded women that believe that," Doctor Roberts explained.

"Shantel, please respond to the concerns that Gerome has."

"Well, what can I say after hearing all of that?" Shantel asked. "I know that we don't make love every day, but I thought that Gerome was at least being satisfied."

"Shantel, how can you think that, if you all only make love on special occasions and holidays? Especially when you all made love more frequently before marriage."

"Baby, please don't think that you don't satisfy me in any area, because you do. But sexually, we need help. A brother's hand gets tired sometime."

"Well, Gerome, why don't you ever say anything?"

"I do, all of the time. Every night when I caress your hair or kiss you on the neck, I am telling you. When I try to wake you up at night, and you just roll over, I'm telling you. When I come out of the shower and lay in bed, I am telling you. But you only turn your back to me. Plus, I verbally tell you that I need some love and affection, but you just brush me off."

"Shantel, have you ever thought about Gerome's needs and desires as a man or your duties as a wife to him sexually?" Doctor Roberts asked.

"I guess I have never really just thought about it. I thought our conversation and our family time was enough to carry him through the times we weren't sexually active. I guess I was wrong."

"Baby, family time and conversation is good, but I have physical needs. A brother's hands are getting tired," said Gerome.

"Shantel, a healthy marriage does consist of family time, conversation, affection, and making love. It's a natural function of the body. I realize because of your past, that sexual intercourse is hard for you. This is why these counseling sessions are so important so your husband can get an understanding and you can receive some healing. Thus, the two of you have a healthy sex life as well," explained the doctor.

"Okay, I guess I understand. Gerome, please forgive me and I will try to do better. I don't know how long it's going to take, but I am willing to go the extra mile to improve and enhance our sex life." Shantel leaned over and whispered in Gerome's ear, "I might even dress up and we can play cops and robbers."

Gerome laughed.

"Alright, you two," the doctor smiled. "Shantel, I have some pamphlets in my briefcase that should help you get over this sexual hump."

"Any help we can get would be great, Doctor. I want Gerome and I to experience marriage to its fullest."

"Yea, baby. Go and get you some of that sexy lingerie and some toys," Gerome laughed.

Shantel nudged his arm.

"If that is all for today, I am going to run. I am surprising my wife today with a trip to Antigua for her birthday," Doc said.

"That's alright, Doctor. Go ahead and take care of your wife. There are a few surprises I have for Shantel too," he winks at her. Doctor Rob leaves.

****

Three months had passed since Kim had her fibroids removed. She and James fought about it all of the time, so she just went forward with the surgery. The doctor had to perform a partial hysterectomy, though.

Kim was not happy with the outcome because the doctor told her she wouldn't be able to have kids. Only a small percentage of women with this type of procedure still get pregnant in their lifetime. Kim was trying to accept what the doctor told her, but she just couldn't handle it. It seemed as if everywhere she went, somebody was pregnant or had recently given birth. With the overwhelming pressure of not being able to conceive, Kim fell into a deep depression. She couldn't stand to look at her husband that she loved so dearly.

James sat on the edge of the bed while Kim packed her clothes. He couldn't believe that his best friend was walking out on their marriage.

"Kim, sweetheart, please reconsider what you're doing. You just can't walk out on me like this."

"James, you forced me to have a surgery that I now regret. I am not going to allow you to force me into raising someone else's child."

"Kimmie, I am only trying to make both of our dreams come true. Our dream is for us to have a family, to raise children together. If we go forward with the adoption, we will be doing just that."

Kim gave James a look of ridicule and said, "James, you can fix it up however you like. I am not raising another woman's child. I want to have my own. Can't you understand that?"

"Can't you understand that God allows everything to happen for a reason. Kimmie, you are not a selfish person. Why not help an innocent child since we are barren?"

"Stop saying that! I am not barren. God promised me children."

"And adopting is God's answer to prayer. He never said how."

Kim sat on the bed next to James. "James, I will love you always.
I hate we are not on one accord on this matter, but I am not going through with it. I am not ready for it, so I hope you can understand. Lele has agreed to let me stay in her guest house until I figure things out."

James grabbed Kim and just held her in his arms. The separation would be very difficult for the both of them. James knew as long as he had that child, Kim would not come back. He wondered if moving forward with the adoption was worth sacrificing his marriage.

James knew he had an extremely difficult decision to make. He loved Kim with everything he had in him. On the other hand, his desire to be a father was equally important.

"James, can you please not move forward with this adoption? Let's just go to a fertility specialist and have further test run," Kim cried.

"Kim, the arrangements have been made and the necessary paperwork has been completed. I pick up little Trinitee tomorrow. Kim, please just give it a chance."

"I can't right now. I won't say never, but not right now. I need some time for me."

"Okay, baby. I have to understand your position. We have never been separated before and it's really going to be hard for me." James paused, "So what do we call this? Will we ever be husband and wife under the same roof again?"

"I pray so, James. This is just one of those times that we just have to trust God and follow our hearts. And our hearts just so happen to be going in different directions. Lele has referred me to a fertility specialist and I am going to make an appointment. I will call you and let you know the results."

"Hey, I am still your husband. Let me know when the appointment is, and I will go with you. Trinitee starts daycare in a week."

"I would really like that, James. I love you," she kissed him and they made love one last time.

****

Monay arrived for yet another round of extensive treatments for her diagnosis. Weeks had passed and Monay had lost more mobility of her limbs. Some days were better than others, though. There were days that her fatigue was too much to bear, and other days it was okay. It fluctuated day to day. Lele accompanied Monay for the majority of her appointments. When Lele couldn't get away, either Kim or Shantel sacrificed time off to be with her.

"Lele, I really want to thank you for being here for me these past few months. You and the girls have shown me what true friendship really means. I know I haven't been the best friend, but you always forgive me and keep it moving. How can I ever repay you for your love?"

"Monay, please. Girl, this is what friends are for. It's all good that we can hang out and eat, but when it really matters, you should be able to count on your friends. You don't have to repay me for anything. The only thing you need to do is get your healing," replied Lele.

"Girl, I am believing for my healing. I am not sure how much longer I can go through these treatments. I'm tired."

"Monay, I just thought of something. There is one thing you can do for me for repayment of all of my time. How about you join me for church service on Sunday? God would really like to meet you there," said Lele.

"Lele, girl, why are you tripping? Now you know God is not thinking about me. He gave up on me a long time ago. That was a good try, though. Anything else you want me to do, I will do it."

"Monay, God has not given up on you or let you go. You went to church sometimes as a child, and you hear me preach it enough. God's Word says that He will never leave us nor forsake us, so try again. I know you think God doesn't care about you anymore, because you have shunned him so many times, but He does. He is just waiting with open arms for your return unto Him."

"We will see, Lele. Don't be worrying me about church while I am on this equipment."

Before she could finish, the doctor walked in.

"Hello, Dr. Mondrake, I see we meet again," he flirted with Lele.

"Hello, Dr. Griffin," Lele said to the specialist.

The two were former coworkers. Dr. Griffin had been asking Lele out for a date for years, even though both were married. She didn't even consider his invitations.

The specialist turned to Monay and said, "Ms. Myers, your body is responding very well to the treatments. With continued treatments, eventually, you could receive full mobility back."

Monay asked, "How long do you think it's going to take? I really need to be getting back to work."

"Ms. Myers, I can't give you a definite timeframe. I can only let you know that we are on the right track.

Things are going well. Only the good Lord above knows your healing." Dr. Griffin winked at Lele and asked, "Isn't that right, Dr. Mondrake?"

Lele quickly coped an attitude. She hated for married men to flirt with her, especially him. "Thanks for the information Dr.," Lele said and showed him the door.

Monay lay on the table about to bust a gut laughing so hard. "Lele, girl, how are you going to put the man out of his own office. You are one bold girl," she laughed.

"Girl, you know I hate to be disrespected. He needs to sit his old married behind down somewhere. He is going to end up catching something."

"Hell, girl, if I wasn't on this table sick, I would give him the time of his life. He would keep coming back for me," laughed Monay.

"Monay, do you hear yourself? That's probably why the Lord had to sit you down with this infirmity in the first place. The only thing you think about is getting with somebody's husband. Do you think the Lord is going to heal you for you to go back and do the same things you have been doing? No, Monay, He is not," said Lele.

"Damn, Lele. Girl, I was just kidding. I was just trying to get my mind off of my problems. I don't need another sermon."

"Oh. I'm sorry, Monay. You know I can't help it. I am going to put forth a conscious effort not to beat you over the head with the bible anymore today," she laughed.

"That should be easy considering we will be leaving soon," Monay giggled.

"So, is this going to be the Sunday you join me in church?" Lele asked.

"Lele, are you experiencing memory loss at an early age?"

"Why do you ask that?"

"Because, in your last breath, didn't you just say you weren't going to beat me over the head with the bible anymore today?"

"Lele laughed, "Girl, I didn't mention the bible. Church is something totally different."

"Aren't you just a smarty pants?" Monay smirked.

"Like you always say, I did attend college," Lele giggled.

"Very funny. I can't make it this Sunday. I start taking shots at home that day. I'm not sure what kind of effect it will have on me."

"Girl, those shots don't have too many side effects. You will probably be weak for a little while, but that's it. So, try something else."

"I'm gonna be too weak, Lele,"

"Okay, well, let's make a deal. You go to church with me, and I will give you your shot after service."

"We will see. I'm not going to make any promises. I'll let you know by Saturday. Deal?"

"That's no kind of deal. I'm not going to harass you about going. I will be at your house by seven. Don't forget I have a key. So I advise you to be ready. If not, I will help you get dressed," Lele laughed.

"Tramp, give me back my house key."

"No, ma'am," Lele laughed.

Moments later, the machine stopped. Lele helped Monay get dressed and she dropped her off at home. Lele went home to meet Darryl.

****

"So Alecia, how is Kim doing these days?" Darryl asked.

"All I can say is that she is holding on. She hardly ever comes out of the guesthouse unless she is going to work or church. She's not eating properly or anything."

"I really hope she and James can work things out," said Darryl.

"James went to a doctor's appointment with her a few weeks ago, so they are still communicating and having conjugal visits," Lele laughed. "Kim has yet to see the baby that James adopted, though. That is really sad, and it just hurts my heart.

"Having a child has to be extremely important for James to disrupt his marriage. But who am I to judge? I am on the outside looking in. If faced with the exact situation, I am not sure what decision I would make."

"Well, I would hope you would choose your wife. At least give her some time before you just go do what you think is best for the both of you."

"Well, it's not our problem, so we won't continue to discuss it. Let's talk about us." Darryl said.

"What about us? Us is just fine," Lele laughed.

"Yes, honey, you are fine," Darryl giggled.

"Alright, boy. Don't you start with me."

"Alecia, when are we going to go shopping for rings?"

"Rings for what?" she asked.

"Girl, stop playing. I have already found my wedding band. I want to take you so I can see how bad you are going to hurt my pockets."

"Uh, did I say I was going to marry you or something? I told you that I would think about it."

"Well, you have thought about it long enough. I think it's time to begin making wedding plans.

"Boy, you are a trip. You are acting like James trying to make your own decisions. I guess we can go. I can show you the three rings that I have picked out."

"Oh, you are ahead of the game, I see," said Darryl.

"Darryl, I was confident in knowing that God was going to bless me, so I wanted to be prepared. Your pockets won't cry too hard. The most expensive one is four karats and only $49, 995. I'm sure you can handle that," suggested Alecia.

"Alecia, you are trying to make a brother pick up a second job, aren't you?"

"If that's too much, I can get another one. That was just my favorite set out of the three. My third choice is a past, present, and future set, and it's only $9,999. Is that better, Mr. Cheapo?" she laughed.

"Who is cheap? Alecia, I was only kidding. You can have whatever your little heart desires. We will go this weekend so you can show me the sets and get your finger sized."

That sounded much better to Alecia. She was gonna be a bit hurt if she couldn't get her favorite set because Darryl was a millionaire. He had been spoiling her rotten since they had been together. But she would have gotten over it though because she truly loved Darryl and not his money. His wealth was just a wink of the eye from the Lord.

"Sounds good. Since you have everything all worked out, what are we going to do about living arrangements?"

"Well, I suggest that we sell your house, and the two of you move out to the ranch. How much longer do you have to pay on your house anyway?" Darryl recommended.

"Sweetie, my house is paid for! We only had a fifteen-year mortgage. Thank God I only have to pay the insurance and the maintenance. With the housing market in shambles like it is today, my house would probably be a statistic," she laughed.

"I wouldn't allow that to happen to you."

"What about all of my furniture?"

"Sweetie, haven't you heard of the salvation army or goodwill?" Darryl laughed. Darryl often made fun of Alecia because he thought she was rather a slow thinker at times.

"Yea, I guess I could do that. But the French leather sofa set has to go to Shantel. She has always liked it. She would have a fit if she found out I gave it away."

"I bet. Then there are some things you can keep in storage for AD. He can have a well-furnished bachelor's pad for his first apartment."

"What do you mean bachelor's pad? My baby will not be anybody's eligible bachelor. AD is my baby!"

"Speaking of a baby. What do you think about us getting pregnant right after the wedding? You know I am getting older, and I would like to have me a couple a kids."

Alecia was speechless. She really had never thought about having any more kids. "It never dawned on me that Darryl would want kids," she thought to herself.

"A couple? You're kidding right? You've never even mentioned children. I can see one baby. We can have a Darryl Jr. plus AD and you have a couple of kids. I also would like for us to wait at least a year before trying so we can really enjoy each other and travel. But if you want to jump right in, I reckon traveling will have to wait."

"Well, Alecia, I did want a boy and girl of my own. What if you have a girl the first time? Then I won't have anyone to carry on my name. Can you understand that?"

"Yes, I understand. We will just pray about it and see what the Lord says. AD will probably be excited about being a big brother." After Lele finished her statement, the phone rang. She looked at the caller id and noticed that it was AD.

"Speaking of my angel. This is AD calling now."

****

"Hey, AD, Darryl and I were just talking about you. How are you, sweetheart?" Alecia asked her son.

"I'm fine, Mom. I'm just calling to let you know that I will be coming home this weekend," AD explained.

Alecia couldn't believe her ears. Ever since AD met Darryl, he had been coming home quite frequently. She figured that was a good thing.

"You're coming home again?" Alecia questioned.

"Yea, that's not a problem, is it?"

"Baby, no. You coming home is never a problem. I am sure Darryl will plan a nice family weekend. Have you purchased your train ticket yet, or should I do it?"

"I've already taken care of it, Mom."

"Okay. AD be sure to bring home the dates you will be home for the summer. Darryl wants to take us to Niagara Falls for summer vacation."

"Well, Mom, I know I told you I would only be home for a few weeks, but I have changed my mind. I will be home for the entire summer. I want me and Big D to hang out more," said AD.

Alecia became speechless after hearing that. AD just kept on surprising her when it came to Darryl.

"Well, AD, that's great. I've missed you so much since you've been gone. Now maybe we can catch up. There are some things I need to discuss with you anyway."

"Okay, Mom. Before you hang up, can I speak to Big D?" asked AD.

"Sure, honey,"

Alecia handed Darryl the phone but still couldn't believe how well the two men in her life were getting along. She knew God was showing her divine favor.

"What's up, man?" Darryl asked.

"Hey, Big D. What are you gonna have planned for the fellas this weekend?"

"I don't know. We will probably go to the ranch and get on the kayaks. How about that?"

"Cool. Can you pick me up from the train station?"

"Yes, sir. I will be there. See you then," Darryl said.

"Alright, Big D. Tell Mom I love her. I will talk to you guys later," AD hung up.

****

"Alecia, AD said he loves you and will talk to you later," Darryl told Alecia.

"Uh, excuse me. He is passing messages I see, huh. I would have liked to tell him goodbye. I'm going to get him when I pick him up."

"Well, babe, you're not picking him up. I am," Darryl said.

"Oh, really? Did he just kick me to the curb? I wonder what that is about."

"Sweetie, it doesn't have to be about anything. My new son just wants to hang with his new daddy. Don't be jealous, baby," Darryl laughed. "Speaking of his daddy, Alecia when are you going to open up about your divorce?"

Alecia had gotten away from that subject for months with Darryl. She knew it would come back up, though. Alecia moved up to the edge of the couch and just looked. She still wasn't ready to talk about that yet but didn't know how much longer she could avoid the subject.

"Darryl, baby, please stop sweating me about my divorce. I am going to tell you when I am ready," she said with attitude.

"Alecia, there is no need to get an attitude about it. I guess I will have to wait until you are ready. I can only pray it's before we get too old."

"I will, Darryl. I don't see what the big deal is about it, but you will know soon. I can make you one promise. I promise you will know everything about my divorce before we get married. Will that work for you?" she asked.

"Yes, sweetie, that will work just fine."

"I do want to thank you for being such an understanding man. I really do appreciate it," she smiled.

Darryl gave Alecia a hug and said, "Hey, baby, I don't want you to feel pressured about anything. So, I won't mention it again. Whenever you are ready, my ears will be listening."

"Oh, Darryl, I just love you so much," Lele smiled.

CHAPTER EIGHT

Girl Time

All of the girls were gathered together at Lele's house for girls' night. They stopped going to Kim's house, of course, since Kim moved out. Monay was on time because she couldn't drive as much, so Lele picked her up. The girls decided to have a cleanup party at Lele's house, so when she moved, they wouldn't have to pack as much.

"I am so glad you all are helping me clean out some of this junk," Lele said.

"You said it right, girlfriend, junk," laughed Monay.

"Monay, you are a mess, girl. Even in your sickness, you still manage to be yourself. CRAZY!" said Shantel.

"Girl, that is the only way for me to remain sane. I never in a million years thought I would be going through something like this. The bible says laughter is medicine for the soul," explained Monay.

"Oh, Lord, you must be on your way back. Do y'all hear Monay quoting scriptures? You have been spending too much time with Lele," laughed Kim.

"Y'all leave my new missionary alone," Lele joked.

"Lele, don't get carried away now. I just started going to church, and you already trying to make me a missionary," said Monay.

Shantel and Kim sat there in amazement. They couldn't believe that Lele didn't tell them that Monay had started going to church with her. Kim was very surprised she didn't know being that she lived with Lele.

"Monay, you been going to church with Lele? Why didn't I know that?" Kim asked.

"Kim, please don't take this wrong, but you would have known if you hadn't stopped going to church," replied Lele.

"Well," laughed Shantel.

"Y'all I have not stopped going to church. I am just taking a sabbatical. God knows I am trying to work some things out before I can go back," said Kim.

"Work some things out? Girl, the only thing that needs working out is your selfishness," said Monay.

"What does that supposed to mean, Monay? I am not selfish."

"You are being selfish. You are only thinking about what Kim wants and not even considering what James want," said Monay.

"No, Monay, James is not the real reason she doesn't want to go back to church. Miss thang does not want to see their new baby," said Shantel.

As they talked, Kim did what she did best. She started to cry as always. The girls didn't care this time. They knew it was time out for all of the foolishness going on with Kim and James.

Lele grabbed some tissue from the bathroom and handed it to Kim.

"Kim, dry up those tears, girley," said Lele.

"So, Kim, is that the real reason you stopped going to church? You don't want to see your new daughter??" asked Monay.

"Would y'all please stop saying that? That is not my daughter. That is James' daughter," replied Kim.

"Trinitee is a very cute little girl. You just wait until you lay your eyes on her. She kind of look like you, Kim," Lele said.

"Well, to be honest with you, I really don't plan on laying my eyes on her if I can help it."

"Kim, I have always expected better from you. That's the trifling way me or Shantel would act. What has gotten into you?" Monay asked. "And when the hell are you going back home? I know Lele is about tired of your ass at her house."

"Excuse me? Monay, please just hush. I do not feel like dealing with your smart comments. I am sure if Lele wanted me out, she would tell me. Right, Lele?"

"That's right, Kim. But you really are going to have to decide what you are going to do. The house will be going up for sale soon. I hope to have it sold before Darryl and I get married," replied Lele.

"Uh and where is your holy roly butt gon' live? I know you are not going to shack up with that man?" asked Monay sarcastically.

"Monay, you are so hilarious. No, I am not going to shack up with that man. Darryl has some vacant rental properties, and he told me that I can live in one of those until we get married."

"Oh, because I was about to read you some scripture," said Monay and everybody laughed.

Everybody knew that if Monay was reading scripture, then something had to be extremely wrong.

"So Lele, you're really going to get married? That must be a special man," Shantel inquired.

"Yes, girls, I think God has sent me my Boaz," Lele smiled.

"You never did tell us what AD thinks about lover man," said Shantel.

"AD just adores him. He actually gets along better with Darryl than I would have ever imagined, especially so soon. He has been coming home more frequently since he met Darryl. They are together tonight. I truly thank God," Lele smiled.

"YES Lord, you are finally about to get you some. Now you can save some money on all of those batteries you buy for that vibrator," laughed Monay.

"So, Lele, have y'all talked about kids?" asked Shantel.

"Yeah, girl. Are you gonna pop out another baby?" asked Monay.

"Yes, we are. Darryl wants to have two children, but we are praying on that one. One would be fine with me," explained Lele.

"Girl, take it from someone who can't get pregnant. If he wants two babies and your body will produce them, go for it. That will give me two more kids to spoil since Shantel's have gotten older," said Kim.

"Kim, this whole baby thing has made you a negative person. You believe for everybody else except yourself. You really used to be the most positive person I have been around," said Shantel. "Why won't you just go back home to your husband and spoil the baby that y'all have adopted?"

"Y'all this is not easy for me. I am tired of saying that to y'all every time we get together.
I miss my husband more and more each day. I am just trying to trust God on this one. I hope one day to move back home with James and start a family. I just don't want to be forced into doing something else that I am against just like my surgery," Kim said.

"Well, you better hope quick, because Lele gon' put you out on the street. You know she don't know how to act with a man. A little piece of the ding dong is going to drive her crazy," chuckled Monay.

"Kim, don't listen to that crazy girl. You are welcome here as long as the house is in my name. I don't know how much longer that's going to be, though. We are shooting to put the house up for sale next month. With the housing market in shambles, it might be on the market a long time. If it doesn't sell, then I will probably rent it out since it's paid for."

"Lele, I didn't know your house was paid for. You be keeping secrets," said Shantel.

"I have been telling y'all that miss holy roly is a little rich girl. Y'all won't listen to me," Monay said.

"Shut up, Monay. There are benefits to tithing," said Lele.

"Lele, if the house is paid for, why sell it in the first place?" asked Kim.

"Well, I don't want to just let the house sit up. It's a beautiful place to raise a family, so it shouldn't be empty."

"Shoot, Lele, if we ever get our finances in order, me and Gerome could rent the house from you. We definitely can't afford to buy it," said Shantel.

"Of course, girl. As long as y'all keep the house in good condition, then y'all could stay as long as you want to. As a matter of fact, if it doesn't sell then you can live here rent-free until you have everything in order. Just pay utilities and the upkeep of the house."

"What?! Lele, are you just going to let that girl and her wild kids live in your house indefinitely? You are better than me," said Monay.

"Shut up old trifling girl. A donkey's behind is better than you," said Shantel.

Monay bust out laughing herself. She knew that she could be quite messy at times. It was all fun and games for her, though. Sometimes the girls got offended by some of the things that she said, but she didn't care. Monay knew that they would get over whatever was bothering them pretty quick.

During their conversation, Kim's phone rang. Everyone knew it had to be James because they all were there.

"Kim, go ahead and answer your phone. You know that's your husband, girl. Answer. We will be quiet. Ask him if you can come home," laughed Monay.

Kim leaned over and looked at the caller id on her cell. Monay was right; it was James calling.

****

"Hey, James," Kim said to James over the phone.

"Hey, baby, how are you?" he asked.

"I'm doing fine. It's girls' night so all of us are here running our mouths as usual. What's going on with you?"

"Nothing. What are you doing tomorrow? I wanted to know if I could stop by since my day is free."

"I have nothing planned. I will be here helping Lele sort out things in the house."

"Okay, that's what I needed to know. I will be over about noon. See you then and I love you."

"I love you too. Goodbye," said Kim and hung up the phone.

As soon as Kim hung up the phone, the girls started ragging her. They knew she missed James so much. Kim sat down on the couch with a huge smile on her face.

"Lord, I miss that man," Kim sighed.

"Kim, that's what you don't get. You don't have to miss him. Go home!" said Shantel.

"What did he say, Kim?" Monay asked.

"He wanted to know what I was doing tomorrow so he could come over. We still try to see each other at least two or three times a week."

"Is he bringing the baby this week? She is such a cutie pie." Lele inquired.

"Girl, no. His mom keeps her when he comes over here. I am still not ready for him to bring her. I can tell it hurts him because I don't want to meet her, but I am hurting too."

"Well, honey, y'all can't live like this forever. It really isn't worth losing a good man over. Y'all had such a good marriage. You are going to have to make a decision soon," said Shantel.

"Because I know you don't want a floosie like me to come and scoop him up. Girl, there are some vultures out there," Monay laughed.

"I know, y'all. If he would just give that baby back and just trust God with me, I will be back home in a flash."

"Now, Kim, just because he adopted that baby don't mean he is not trusting God. James is still going to appointments with you and is very supportive. You are just not being fair," said Lele. "I have been trying to keep quiet and just let you work through everything. James tries to be very understanding about everything, but you're just not thinking rationally. Maybe you all should see that counselor that is helping Shantel and Gerome," said Lele.

"That would be a great idea, Kim. Dr. Roberts has helped us tremendously with all of our issues. Gerome and I are even making love twice a week now. Of course, he would prefer it every day, but change takes time. So, I recommend that the two of you discuss it. I was totally against opening up to a complete stranger about my personal life, but I am so glad I did. If I hadn't, I would probably be living here with Lele too."

"Counselor? Lele, I thought you supported my decision. I thought you understood," Kim mocked.

"Kim, girl, now you know I don't support you leaving your husband. I do support your act of stepping out on faith and holding God accountable to His word, but that's it. I allow you to live here because I love you, and I thought that you would have heard from God by now."

"Lele, I hear from God every day. You aren't the only one that can hear from Him. I see where our friendship stands. I will start looking for an apartment next week, so I can get out of your hair."

"Kim, don't even try to question my friendship to you. All of us know that this is not about friendship or anything else. Don't avoid the real issue. This is about Kimberly Brister. I won't allow you to turn this around and blame me for your problems. I have enough of my own," Lele said angrily.

"Whew, it's about to get crunk in here. I needs me some whiskey," chuckled Monay.

"Girl, you better sit your recovering behind down somewhere. You know you are not allowed to drink with that medication," said Shantel.

"Shantel, I know that. I needs me a drank and a man. It has been months since I have whipped me a man. I am going into withdrawal. Those two ingredients are a necessity for me to live day to day. Don't you see me shaking over here," Monay laughed.

"Well, y'all it's getting late. I think I better head on home to Gerome and the kids. We have a big day tomorrow. We are going to sit down and discuss a few possible business ventures that could be profitable enough to get us back on track financially. It's a thin line between where we are right now financially and poverty," said Shantel.

"Well, since it's so late, Lele, I am going to just spend the night. You can take me home tomorrow," said Monay.

Kim continued to sit over in the corner, upset with her lip poked out. She couldn't believe nobody could understand what she was going through. Inside, she knew the things they were telling her were the right things, but she just didn't want to hear it. "I just feel so alone, God. Nobody understands," Kim thought to herself.

"I guess you can stay one night," Lele laughed. "We can have a slumber party. I will go get some movies and blankets. We can stay up all night."

"Oh, y'all wanna have a sleepover when you know I can't stay. Y'all so dirty. I'm gone. I will talk to y'all tomorrow some time," Shantel left out of the door.

"Y'all I don't really feel like watching movies tonight. I hope y'all don't mind if I head back to the guest house," Kim stated.

"Kim, don't go. Girl, come and stay because you know it's going to be fun. Especially when Monay start slobbering out of the mouth," Lele laughed.

"Go to hell, Lele," Monay shouted. "If Kim wants to go and have herself a pity party, let her go. Have a good time letting the devil whip on you, Kim."

Kim must have really gotten mad at Monay's comment. She grabbed her shoes and slammed the door leaving out of the house. Kim had taken all she could handle. She knew she definitely couldn't listen to smart comments for the remainder of the night.

"Girl, I believe we have pissed Kim off for the night. I hope she knows that we love her and only have her best interest in mind," said Lele.

"Whatever. We all have been pissed off at each other before, and we always get over it. She will be alright. Lele, give me a couple of blankets. I think I am going to head to bed. You know you're pretty boring by yourself," she laughed.

KIA STOKES

CHAPTER NINE

The Day After

Kim sat on the couch in the guesthouse, waiting on James to arrive. She knew that once they embraced, she would feel so much better. Although Kim felt that the girls hurt her feelings the night before, she was grateful to them for opening up her eyes to some things. Kim stood up to fix a sandwich, when she noticed James pulling up outside. So she cracked the door open so he could come right in.

As Kim made her way to the kitchen, she heard James talking to somebody on his way in. When she turned around, she could not believe her eyes. James walked in with Trinitee, the little girl he had adopted. Kim's face turned red. Her eyes welled up with tears. That was the first time she had ever laid eyes on Trinitee.

Kim's first reaction was to get upset because James brought her with him, but she couldn't. For the first time, Kim realized that Trinitee was just an innocent child.

James closed the door behind him and said, "Kim, please listen before you start going off on me."

Kim didn't part her lips. She just stood there as James talked.

"I know you told me not to ever bring Trinitee over here, but I had no choice this time. Momma canceled on me at the last minute, so there was nothing for me to do. I really wanted to see you today, and I did not want to disappoint you by not coming. We won't stay long because I don't want you to be forced to interact with Trinitee. And I don't want Trinitee to feel unwanted. So please, can you just give us thirty minutes to spend some time with you, and then we will be out of your hair?" asked James.

Kim just stood there in shock. She knew she really hadn't ever seen such a beautiful baby. Trinitee had beautiful milky way skin, big beautiful eyes, and thick curly hair.

When she smiled, Kim could see one deep dimple embedded in her right cheek.

Kim wiped her tears and said, "Sure, James, please sit down."

"Are you alright? I don't want this to be too much for you."

"I must admit at first I wanted to lash out at you when I saw the baby, but I couldn't. My God James, she is so beautiful." Kim wept.

"Yes, Kim, she is beautiful, just like her mother," he smiled at Kim.

"James, please don't say that."

Trinitee sat in James' lap, just smiling at Kim. At one point, Trinitee reached up at Kim, but she walked away.

"James, what happened to her parents? How could someone leave such a beautiful baby at an orphanage?"

James wanted to tell her the same way that she left, but he knew that wasn't a positive thing to say. "Well, Kim, Trinitee's parents are both dead. One rainy day they were on their way from church, and their vehicle hydroplaned and hit a ravine.

The dad died at the scene and the mother died two days later in the hospital. The doctors managed to save Trinitee. She was in the hospital for three months. None of their family were in a position to raise her, so she ended up at the orphanage."

"That is such a sad story. Poor thing. Do you want a sandwich or something to drink?"

"No, we ate before we left home. Thanks for offering, though. I do need to run to the bathroom really quick. I am going to sit Trinitee right here on the floor. Can you watch her for a minute to make sure she doesn't get into any of your things?"

"James, I don't know about that," she hesitated.

"The only thing you have to do is keep your eye on her. I won't be gone but two minutes."

"Okay, but you better come right back. Don't forget to wash your hands. You don't want to transfer germs to the baby," she laughed.

"Girl, hush. You know I am not a nasty man."

Kim sat there and watched Trinitee while she crawled around playing. Minutes passed and James still wasn't out of the bathroom.

So, Kim decided to check on him. "James, did you fall in the toilet or something?" she yelled.

"No. My stomach is running off. I'll be out shortly," James grunted.

"Okay, make sure you spray some air freshener with your stanky self. You're in there blowing up my bathroom," Kim laughed.

Trinitee continued to play and Kim chased her around the living room. When Kim sat back down, Trinitee crawled over and reached out to her. "Lord, what am I supposed to do now?" she asked herself.

Trinitee continued to reach and began to cry when Kim wouldn't pick her up. James yelled from the bathroom he would be out shortly. Kim couldn't stand to see Trinitee cry, so she picked her up. "Here we go," Kim sighed.

Kim leaned over and grabbed Trinitee from the floor. At that moment, Kim fell in love with her. Trinitee giggled and laid her head in Kim's chest. Kim thought that everything about that picture felt right to her. The feeling she longed for; she began to feel. Kim hummed a nursery rhyme until James returned.

"Hey, sorry I took so long. That sweet and sour chicken tore my stomach up. What are you girls in here doing?" James asked in a shocking manner. He could not believe that Kim was holding Trinitee. Although that was something that he fervently prayed for, he never thought that would have happened the first time they met.

"Nothing really. Trinitee started to cry because she wanted me to hold her."

"I'll take her now," replied James.

"That's alright, James. She is settled and on her way to sleep. I wouldn't want to interrupt her naptime."

"Okay, fine with me. I am enjoying this picture. It's awesome to see. Kimmie, how do you feel holding our little girl?"

Kim hesitated and said, "James, I feel a mixture of emotions. Some of them feel right, and some of them don't. I don't know what to feel."

"Talk to me about it."

"Give me a minute. Let me go and lay Trinitee in my bed."

"You don't have to do that. We can lay her right here on the couch."

"No, it's fine. I will be right back."

When Kim came back, she sat down on James' lap.

"James, Trinitee is so adorable. I could just keep her forever."

"Kim, you can keep her forever. The adoption is complete, and she is ours. We are waiting on you.

"I know James. I can't lie to you and tell you that while holding her, I didn't feel like I was her mother. When she looked up at me with those beautiful eyes, my heart melted away. I love her already, and I just met her. I just don't know if I am ready yet, though."

"What do you have to be ready for? It will be just like we had given birth to her ourselves. Come on, Kim. Just give it a try and come home. You know how much I miss you. I miss your touch and your warm body next to mine," he said and kissed Kim.

"James it's just not that easy. I am going to need some time to think about it. Can you understand that?"

"Yes, baby, I understand. Kiss me. My body is yearning for you."

Kim jumped up to make sure Trinitee was sound asleep. Then she leaned over and kissed James on his neck. It had been so long for James, he jumped right out of his clothes.

In the middle of them making love, Trinitee woke up crying. Kim tried to jump up to go and check on her, but James said, "Baby, she will be alright."

"James, boy, I have to go check on her," said Kim. She threw on her shirt and ran to the bedroom. She came back with Trinitee.

"I guess she took a catnap," said Kim. "Hey, my little tinkerbell," she said to Trinitee jumping her on her lap. "James, get up and put your clothes on."

"I'm already up. I was trying to get down, but Trinitee woke up," he said sarcastically. "It's getting late. We better get back across town anyway."

"Y'all can stay a little while longer."

"It's already after six, and I have to give Trinitee her bath and get her ready for bed. You know we are 45 minutes away from here."

"Do you have enough milk and diapers with you that will last until tomorrow?" asked Kim.

"Sure, I do. I keep extra everything in the trunk. Why, what's up?"

"I'm probably really about to blow your mind. I was thinking that maybe the two of you could spend the night. You would have to sleep on the couch, though. The bed is only a full size and that is not big enough for the three of us."

"You're kidding, right? Are you serious?" asked James in disbelief.

"Yes, I'm serious. Let's just see what happens. I really want to be a family again."

Kim put in a movie, and the three cuddled up together on the couch until they fell asleep.

****

Lele and AD pulled into the garage. She was returning from picking him up from boarding school. AD decided to spend the entire summer at home and Lele was looking forward to it.

"Momma, I'm so glad I'm home for the summer," AD said to Lele.

"Me too, AD. I've missed you so much since you've been gone," Lele agreed. "You will have the summer to finish packing up the game room and your bedroom."

"What am I packing for, Mom? Are we moving somewhere, and you forgot to tell me?"

"Come on inside so we can talk," Lele smiled.

AD put his suitcase on the kitchen floor and sat down at the table.

"Do you want some juice, honey?" she asked AD.

"Sure, Mom. Some V-8 if we have any."

"Of course, we have some," she smiled. Lele grabbed a can of V-8 from the fridge and handed it to AD. She sat down at the table across from him.

"Sweetheart, Darryl and I have become very close these past few months. We've grown to love one another. When two people fall in love the way we have, there comes a time that you have to take the relationship to another level. I guess what I'm trying to say is …," Lele hesitated.

AD interrupted and said, "You're trying to say what, Mom? That you're getting married?"

"Yes, AD. Yes. Darryl and I are getting married. We're not officially engaged yet, though. How do you feel about that?" she asked reluctantly.

Lele was confident that AD and Darryl had a good relationship, but she didn't know how he would feel with a man living under the same roof with them.

"That's great, Mom. I really like Big D and I know he loves you. The night you were having girls' night, he asked my permission to marry you. So, I've been expecting this conversation."

Lele threw a napkin at AD. "So, you knew already? Darryl didn't even mention that he had spoken to you about it. I've been fasting and praying every day trying to figure out how to tell you, and you already knew." She wiped sweat from her forehead.

"I must admit, it was rather funny watching you sweat," AD laughed.

"Boy, that wasn't funny. You shouldn't taunt your mother in that way. You know how important it is to me that you're comfortable with everything," Lele smiled.

AD winked at his mother and said, "I know, Mom."

He paused and said, "There is something I would like to discuss with you."

"What is it, son?"

"I think I am ready to move back home."

"You mean like permanently?" Alecia asked.

"Yes, Mom."

"Really, son? That's great. What made you come to that decision?" she asked in shock.

"Well, I have missed home for some time now, but just never mentioned it. I really enjoy being with Big D. So, once I come home, our family will be complete."

"Well, I don't know about complete."

"What do you mean?" AD asked.

"Well, Darryl and I have been talking, and we have decided to have another child."

"A baby?"

"Yes, Addonte.' You have always wanted to be a big brother," Lele reminded him.

"Hmmm. Let me think about it." He paused. "I thought about it. I think it will be fun to have a sister or brother to beat up on," he laughed.

Alecia laughed.

"So, when do you want to move home?"

"I was thinking like, now. I was thinking that Big D could drive the truck and move all of my things."

"That soon, huh?"

"Why prolong it?" he laughed.

"Okay, well, I will go on Monday and have you enrolled back into the academy."

"Sounds good. I'm going to call Big D and tell him the good news," he kissed his mother.

****

"How are the two of you today?" Doc Rob asked.

"Never better, Doc," Shantel smiled.

"I'm glad to hear that. The two of you have completely turned your marriage around for the better. …I think my journey with you has come to an end."

"Doc Rob, I can't thank you enough for intervening to help us save our marriage. We don't even fight anymore, but instead, we have civilized conversations. Not so long ago, I remember I was ready to give Shantel over to the dogs," Gerome smiled.

"Boy, that's if I hadn't put you on the curb first," she laughed.

"To hear you all, laugh and joke together is such a sweet melody to my ears," Doc said.

"Doc, we have some more good news for you," said Shantel.

"Gerome and I have decided to start that catering business he has always dreamed of."

Doc Rob grinned. "Now what do you say? That is some very exciting news. I want to be your first client. I want to have an appreciation dinner for my staff next week. Do you think you can create a nice menu and serve it at such a late notice?"

"Of course, we can," Shantel smiled. "Doctor, I am really grateful for your help. There had been so many times that I wanted to just die because of my childhood. I didn't feel Gerome loved me and the list goes on. You've heard this all before. But when God allowed you to minister to me right where I was hurting, I received my healing. I'm no longer bound by my past," a tear fell. Shantel grabbed Gerome's hand, "Doctor, you have changed my life forever. If there is any way we can repay you, you got it. Thanks so much."

"It has been my pleasure. The most important thing to remember is to communicate, stay focused on God, and love each other. Okay?"

"Okay."

"One more thing. I host two marriage workshops a year, and they would serve as a refresher course for you. I would like to invite you to them," Doc Rob said.

"We would love to come. We could share our testimony to other couples," Gerome said.

"Very good then. Well, I better be going. I'm serious about catering my event. Gerome, stop by the office and pick up the check."

"I sure will. Thanks again, Doc."

Doc Rob grabbed his briefcase and said, "I wish you all the best." Then he left.

CHAPTER TEN

Long Time Coming

Weeks passed and Kim spent more and more time with James and Trinitee. James would bring Trinitee over all of the time. Then there were days that Kim would visit unexpectedly just to bring Trinitee a little surprise or something. After much praying and fasting, Kim decided to move back home. She decided not to tell James, though. She wanted to surprise him one day. The only thing she took with her to Lele's house was her clothes anyway. So, she figured that she would just pack her trunk and show up in a few days.

Before Kim could put her plan into motion, James came down with the flu. One day James called Kim and asked her to pick up a prescription the doctor called in because he wasn't feeling well. Of course, she drove right over to take care of him and to make sure that Trinitee was alright. When she arrived, she found the two laid out on the floor watching cartoons. She handed James his prescription and fixed him some water and a can of soup. Then she picked Trinitee up and gave her a big hug.

"Oh, James, baby didn't you get your flu shot this year?" she asked James.

"No, I forgot. I didn't have you here to remind me and it didn't even cross my mind. The doctor has taken me off work for two weeks. I don't want to pass the virus to Trinitee, so I've been spraying Lysol like crazy. Would you mind taking her home with you for a week or so or until I am up and running again," he asked.

Kim smiled. "Sure James, I guess I can help you out this time. Who have you been around picking up flu germs anyway?"

"A couple of guys from work had had it a few weeks ago. I guess I got it from them. Luckily, Trinitee hasn't caught it."

"Have you taken Trinitee for her flu shot?" Kim asked.

No, it hadn't even crossed my mind. I didn't know children her age could get them anyway."

"I promise you can't do anything without me," Kim smiled.

"I shouldn't have to. That's why God created helpmeets, but since I am a single parent, I lack some things," he laughed. "I can't think of everything."

Kim gave James' head a slight nudge and said, "Big Head." Trinitee laughed and slobber ran from her mouth.

****

Kim took the entire week off so she could be home with Trinitee. Over the next week, Kim and Trinitee bonded a great deal. Kim cried every night because, in her heart, she still longed to give birth to her own child. Although Trinitee couldn't fill that void in her heart, she still enjoyed being a mother to her. Kim accepted that maybe this was just the way God wanted it to be.

After James recovered from the flu, Kim took Trinitee back home. James was on the porch waiting for the two of them when she drove up. Kim could hardly park the car because James ran into the driveway.

"Boy, move out of the way so I can park," Kim honked the horn.

James stepped onto the grass as Kim parked the car. James hugged Kim and unbuckled Trinitee's car seat to pick her up. The three went into the house.

"I see you have all of your energy back, mister."

"Yes, Lord. I cannot get sick again. That was a horrible experience to go through alone," replied James.

"Boy, you weren't alone. Jesus was with you," Kim giggled.

"Kimmie, you know what I'm saying," he looked into her eyes.

"I know James. I miss you too, but let's not talk about that right now. Can you go get Trinitee's bags out of the trunk?"

"When are we going to talk about it, Kim?" James asked.

"Later. Just go and get the things from the trunk."

James sighed and went to the car. Kim stood at the door. He opened the trunk and it was filled with all of Kim's suitcases.

"Kim, have you been living out of your trunk?" he asked.

"No. What do you take me for? I have too many friends for me to be living on the street. Besides, God always provides for me," she replied.

"Well, why is your luggage in the trunk miss smarty pants," he asked sarcastically.

"You're intelligent. Figure it out," Kim laughed

James stood there. Then his mouth dropped and his eyes opened wide. "Is this what I think this is, Kimmie?"

"It depends," she smiled. "What do you think?"

"Are you coming back home?!"

She stepped on the porch and said, "I guess so." Then she smiled.

James dropped everything and ran to Kim. He picked her up in his arms and swung her around. "Hallelujah! Thank you, Jesus! Thank you, Jesus! Girl, I love you," he kissed her. "I knew my God wasn't going to take you away from me. Welcome home, baby. Welcome home."

"I'm glad to be back. It was cold in that bed at night without you."

James put Kim down and ran around the front yard screaming. Kim grabbed Trinitee from the living room and brought her outside.

"Trinitee, do you see your daddy running around like a crazy man? Huh, do you see him?"

Trinitee giggled. She looked at Kim and said, "Mommy. Mommy."

A tear dropped down Kim's face. She had always yearned to hear those words. She squeezed Trinitee really tight and replied, "Yes, daughter. I am your mommy. Mommy loves you so much."

James finally calmed down and ran back to the porch. "Kimmie, why are you crying?"

"Trinitee called me Mommy."

James hugged Kim and Trinitee. "God is good, isn't he? He always answers our prayers in His own way. My family is back together again. That is definitely something for me to cry about."

KIA STOKES

CHAPTER ELEVEN

Surprise

"Hey, Mom, some friends are coming to pick me up so we can go skating. Is that alright?" AD yelled upstairs to his mother.

"Sure, honey. Just be home by curfew," Lele yelled back.

"Curfew? Mom," he whined.

"Yes, curfew, mister. Ten o'clock. Leave the porch light on. Darryl is coming over."

Moments later, AD heard a horn outside. His friends were there to pick him up. Before he left, AD let Darryl in the house without telling his mom.

Lele came downstairs and went into the kitchen to fix some lemonade. When she looked up, Darryl was standing there.

Lele was startled.

"Boy," she pushed him. "How did you get in here?"

"My son let me in," he smiled.

"Very funny. Don't scare me that way," Lele walked into the living room. "So, what movie do you want to watch tonight?"

"How about we make our own movie," Darryl laughed.

"Keep dreaming."

"What about that new movie we bought, "Unbound"? Darryl suggested.

"Yes, let's watch that one," Lele agreed.

Lele put in the movie while Darryl grabbed some cookies and milk from the kitchen. She noticed a new throw pillow on the couch.

"Darryl, this is a really nice pillow. I'm sure you brought it to add to my collection," she said.

"Aren't we just a little know it all. Yes, honey, it's yours. Where is the remote so we can start the movie?"

They laughed and cried while they watched the movie. At the end of the movie, there was a wedding.

"See, Darryl, that is such a beautiful ceremony. I would love that color scheme whenever we get married," she said sarcastically.

"Whenever?" he asked. "What does that supposed to mean?"

"Well, I am not rushing you or anything, but I thought I would have my ring by now. Shantel and her family will be moving in soon. I would like to have a ring before me, and AD move into your vacant property."

"How do you know I don't have your ring already, Miss Prissy Ann?"

"With you having it is not benefiting me any," she smirked.

"Alecia, I believe I detect a little attitude," he laughed.

Lele nudged him on the shoulder.

"Pass me your new pillow," Darryl said.

"For what? Don't change the subject, Darryl."

"Girl, just get the pillow," he demanded.

Lele picked up the pillow from the couch, and a tiny pink bag dropped to the floor.

Darryl sat there with his eyebrow raised, and his hand propped up to his face.

"What is this," she wondered.

Lele picked the bag up. She tried to figure out what was inside by feeling the bag, but she couldn't. She threw the pillow at Darryl and sat down beside him. Darryl placed his index finger on Lele's face and lifted up her chin. Then he grabbed the bag from Lele's hand.

"You know I love you, don't you?" he smiled at her while opening the bag.

"What does love have to do with it, Ike?" she laughed.

Darryl then pulled out a ring. It was a princess cut centered diamond surrounded by baguettes and crushed diamonds. It glistened like a star in the midnight sky. Lele's eyes immediately filled with tears. She placed both of her hands to cover her face.

"Don't try to be all shy now. Uncover your face," he took Lele's hands down.

"Oh, Darryl," she said.

"He grabbed her hand and placed the ring on her finger.

She started stomping her feet.

"Jesus!! Thank you, Jesus!"

Darryl picked Lele up and sat her on his lap. He gently kissed her lips.

"The bible says, 'he that findeth a wife findeth a good thing.' After a long goose hunt." He smiled. "I believe I have found the only good thing. Alecia, will you do me the honor of being my wife?"

Lele grinned and said, "Of course I will, Mr. Chocolate."

Then she laid a wet sloppy kiss on him.

"Boy, I love you so much."

"Hey, what's not to love about me?"

Lele suddenly jumped up.

"Where is my phone? I need to call the girls!"

"You can call the girls after I leave. I want us to enjoy this moment right now," Darryl suggested.

"Sure thing, my fiancé," she giggled.

Lele grabbed her day planner and sat next to Darryl.

"Are you about to record this date?" Darryl asked.

"No," she replied.

"Well, what are you doing?"

"You'll see," she smiled.

Then she pulled out a green slip of paper with a long list of items on it.

"What is that, girl?"

"These are our wedding plans."

"Our wedding plans? I don't remember us discussing any details other than the month and possible venues?"

"Well, these are the things that I came up with. I am sure you will agree to them," she assured Darryl.

"Oh, so you were just waiting on me," he laughed.

"Exactly! It took you long enough. But as beautiful as this ring is, it was well worth the wait. I can't believe you bought the ring that I wanted. You really do love me," she kissed his nose.

"I was thinking that our colors could be pink and green. I only have three bridesmaids and AD is going to give me away. Since we have already looked at the venue site for the wedding and reception, planning will be easy."

"Alecia, whatever your heart desires is fine with me. The smile you have right now is the only thing I want to see that day and to wake up to for the rest of my life. So, if you want to come in on a helicopter or boat, you can do it."

"Whew! Boy, stop trying to seduce me," she chuckled.

"I'm serious. And I have something else for you."

"I don't need anything else, baby. I have God, AD, you, and a few good friends. I couldn't be any happier."

"I wanted to do something else nice for you," he smiled.

"Ok, Darryl, what is it?"

"Well, I have a couple of things. I need you to call the owner of the venue for the wedding and tell her the exact date of our wedding. Any date you decide is fine with me. As one of my gifts to us, I have already paid for the venue, food for three hundred guests, transportation for us, the bridal party, and once we lock in the date, the hotel will be blocked. All of the rooms are paid for as well for our friends and family. All I want you to be concerned about is looking beautiful for your day. I have the receipts for everything in case you need them."

Lele stood up. "You have done what?!! Really?" tears flowed down her face. "I can't believe this. You have done all of this for me?"

"Yes, Alecia. Isn't that how a king is supposed to treat his queen?"

"Well, I guess it is. I am one favored child of God. I feel like Queen Esther," she smiled.

"Alecia, you deserve everything that God is blessing you with in this season," Darryl replied.

"Wait until the girls hear all of this!" she exclaimed.

"You can go ahead and get your four-way call going on. I need to stop by Derrell's. He is waiting on me to share your reaction to everything."

"I can't believe he didn't spill the beans as much as he talk," she laughed.

"I didn't tell him until this morning. We all know he can't hold anything for a long period of time. The only other person that knew was AD."

"I am going to get that boy. I can't believe my own child is keeping secrets from me. At least it was a good secret," Lele smiled.

Darryl winked at her and said, "I will talk to you later. I love you."

"I love you too," Lele hugged him and he left.

Lele grabbed her cell phone. She called all of the girls and told them she had an emergency and needed them to come over right away.

****

All of the girls arrived at Lele's house. Monay had rollers still in her hair. "Lele, this better be good, girl. I left the salon to come over here. My hair still ain't dry yet. What is your emergency?" Monay fussed.

"Ahhhhhh! Ahhhhh! Woohoo!!!" Lele jumped up and down.

"Lele, stop screaming and tell us what's wrong," said Kim.

"Nothing is wrong, y'all. Everything is so right." Lele threw up her left hand and said, "Am I blinding you all? Darryl and I are engaged!!!!"

"Shut the front door," Shantel said.

All of the girls screamed and jumped, ran and shouted.

"Rich boy spent a lot of money on that ring miss thang," Monay said. "It ain't nothing like any of the rings I've been given," she laughed.

"Monay, you are plain stupid. All of the rings that you were engaged with were not even close to this type of quality. They got that mess from the cracker jack box," Kim responded.

"Y'all forget all of that. We need to CELEBRATE!" Shantel yelled. "A girls vacation is definitely in order for such a celebration. Anybody up for Turks and Caicos?" asked Lele.

"When can we leave?" Kim laughed.

"Turks and Caicos is not in my budget right now. Gerome and I are just getting the catering business going and trying to get ready to move in here, Lele. So, can we just drive somewhere close?" asked Shantel.

"Shantel, girl, please. We have been waiting so long for a moment like this, my hair has turned gray. Don't you see this rinse on my scalp?" Monay chuckled.

"You don't have to worry about money, Shantel. And the rest of you don't, either. I will pay for everything. Can everybody get away next weekend?" asked Lele.

"See! Now that's what I am talking about. It's good to have rich friends," Monay laughed.

"Girl, shut up with your crazy self," Kim said. "I am ready to hit the friendly skies at all times. James and Trinitee need some father-daughter time."

"Okay, great. I will call my travel agent in the morning and make reservations. Look at what my God has done. I still can't believe it."

"I think we need a drink. Kim, get us some glasses. I will grab the wine," Monay said.

Lele stared at Monay.

Monay laughed and said, "Girl, don't look at me like that. The bible didn't say we couldn't drink."

"I will put in our favorite movie for the last time. We can finally exhale now," said Shantel.

"Amen, Shantel. Amen."

KIA STOKES

CHAPTER TWELVE

Revealing Hurt

A couple of weeks later, the girls were off. After a ten-hour flight, the girls landed in Turks and Caicos for their four-day weekend adventure. Lele paid for everyone's all-inclusive vacation, which included a room at a beachfront resort as a gift for participating in her wedding. Kim was overly excited that they made it because she was sick the entire flight. The stewardess ended up moving her seat close to the rear bathroom. Kim had flown many times before long distances. She didn't understand why that particular flight made her sick.

When they made it to the baggage claim area, a greeter was there waiting on them with a sign that read, "Welcome Mondrake Bridal Party."

So Lele told the gentlemen who they were, and he whisked them off to the resort where they would be staying.

Upon arrival at the resort, a concierge team met them at the shuttle to get their luggage. They didn't have to check-in at the front desk because everything had been prepaid. The girls walked into their room and everybody's mouth dropped open. They could not believe the immaculate view through the window. The 3-level suite was spacious and had all of the amenities one would desire. It even had a swim upriver entrance to the room. The girls changed into their bathing suits. Then they grabbed their sunglasses and big floppy hats and left for the beach.

The waves on the beach were high and the surfers were riding the waves. The sand was white and beautiful.

"Whew, Lele, girl, you have really outdone yourself this time. I'm so glad the Lord blessed me with rich friends," Monay laughed.

"You're right, Monay. It will be a miracle if Gerome and me ever get to come and experience something like this.

Lord, speaking of Gerome, I hadn't even called him to tell him we made it," said Shantel.

"Shantel, just give it some time. Y'all business is just getting started. I'm sure in no time, y'all will be flying around the world catering for the rich and famous," Kim reassured her.

"Hey, y'all look at that old couple walking over there," Lele noticed.

Monay laughed, "They look like they are about eighty years old."

"Even if they are, I bet they are still in love. Look at how that man is gripping her around her waist. She is just throwing those hips and smiling as if she just found out someone left her an inheritance," chuckled Kim. "I hope James and I are that happy when we grow old."

"Ditto, Kim. Darryl and I are going to be like them. We can be eighty-five and are still going to get it on as if we are twenty. Darryl might have to become friends with Viagra, though," Lele laughed.

"Oh, Lele, you are wrong for that. That man might still have stamina," said Monay.

While the girls sat on the beach enjoying the sun and talking, a mobile sand buggy rolled by. It offered all types of water sports, including snorkeling. None of the girls had ever been snorkeling before but talked about trying it back home.

"Hey, are y'all ready to try snorkeling today?" asked Lele.

"Nope, girl, we just got here. The first day of a vacation is supposed to be a relaxation day," said Monay.

"Girl, we are only here for four days. We don't have time to relax," said Shantel.

Lele yelled for the buggy to stop so they could go check out the snorkeling schedule. The salesperson didn't hear Lele's soft voice, so they all ran behind the buggy. The sand buggy was moving so slow; it didn't take much out of them to catch up with it. When they got to the window, Monay went off on the man telling him he knew he heard them yelling. The salesman politely apologized to them and offered them a ten percent discount off of their purchase. All of the girls shook their head at Monay.

Shantel commented about how every time they went somewhere with Monay, they always managed to get a discount or something free for complaining.

All of the snorkeling times for that day had passed. So Lele had snorkeling for all of the girls arranged for the private snorkeling reef. She also paid for Monay to ride a jet ski. None of the other girls had enough nerve to try that.

"Okay, girl, since we can't go snorkeling until tomorrow, let's head back to the room," said Lele.

"Yea, I'm hungry," replied Kim.

"I don't see how you are hungry Kim because you ate during the entire flight. You keep on eating, your size six is going to turn into double digits," laughed Monay.

"I could eat something myself. The hotel restaurant seems like it is nice and it's free," said Shantel.

"That's right, Shantel. Food and drinks are included in our package. We even have twenty-four-hour room service for our late nights," said Lele.

The girls went back to the suite, changed clothes, and went downstairs to the restaurant.

The restaurant was very extravagant. Instead of there being a centerpiece on the table, there was a computerized menu listing. They could browse through the menu and place their order right from the table.

"Hello, ladies. I am Enrique, and I will be serving you this evening. Can I start you all with a nice glass of wine," the server asked.

"Hey, there, Enrique. I'll take an apple sour with a shot of you," Monay flirted.

"Monay, don't you start with your hot behind. You are already getting back to your old ways," said Shantel.

"Enrique, a glass of water for everybody," Lele laughed.

"I don't want any water. Bring me an apple martini with salt and water for everybody else," Monay demanded.

Enrique smiled and, in a seductive tone, said, "It is my pleasure."

After he walked away, Monay reapplied her makeup.

"Girl, you should really stop. You still haven't learned your lesson."

"Girl, God didn't say we couldn't look our best. I have to be ready when my Boaz come. I never know where the blessing is coming from," chuckled Monay.

"I heard that, Monay," Kim smiled. "I'm just glad you're no longer a slut."

All of the girls laughed.

"Haters. Y'all are just some old haters," Monay replied.

The girls ordered their food and reminisced on how they first met and all of their past adventures and altercations with one another.

"God has brought us through so much y'all," Lele said.

"Yes, He has," Kim replied and buttered a slice of toast to eat. As soon as she took a bite of the toast, she vomited everywhere.

"Oh, my God, Kim," Shantel yelled.

"What the hell is wrong with you, girl?" Monay asked.

The manager ran to the table with towels to clean the mess.

Lele guided Kim to the restroom.

"Now I can't believe this girl has messed up my first night here. I have lost my appetite," Monay complained. "I need another drink."

"Can you cancel our orders, please?" Shantel asked Enrique who was standing at the table.

"Are you sure you don't want it to go?" he asked.

"No, we will probably just grab some sandwiches from the pub," Shantel replied.

Shantel and Monay were heading to the restroom when they noticed Lele and Kim coming out.

"I'm sorry about that, y'all," Kim apologized. "I don't know what is wrong with me."

"I do. Girl, I think you are pregnant. You know I have a test in the room," Monay laughed, and they headed out.

After they made it back to their suite, Monay whips out a *Find Out Now* pregnancy test.

"Here you go, Kim. You need to go check yourself out," Monay said.

"Kim, you and James must have jumped right in bed nonstop once you moved back in," Shantel commented.

"Yes, ma'am," Kim laughed. "But I can't be pregnant. After the in vitro didn't work, I said I wasn't going to worry about trying to conceive. I told God that I would try to raise Trinitee as my daughter and be satisfied."

"Well, something is going on with you," said Lele.

"Yep, now go take this test, chick," Monay demanded. Kim snatched the test from Monay and went to the bathroom.

"I don't even know why Kim is lying to herself. She knows Trinitee can't satisfy her desire to experience childbirth," Shantel said.

"Shantel, that's not true. Her desire is to be a mother and that's what she is to Trinitee."

After a few moments passed, the girls heard an all-familiar sound. Kim was in the bathroom screaming again. Then she came running down the hall, waving the pregnancy test in the air. Kim's face had turned a cherry color and tears were flowing down her smooth chubby cheek.

She opened her mouth really wide and shouted, "I see a cross! I see a cross! And it's not the one Jesus died on! Y'all I'm pregnant! I'm pregnant! I need to call my husband."

All of the girls leaped into the air. They ran to Kim so they could have a group hug.

"Are you serious?!" Lele hugged. "Look at my God. He's able to do all things," she sang.

"I am so happy for you, Kim. I really am," Shantel commented.

"I knew you were pregnant eating up everything," Monay laughed.

The girls settled down and Monay popped the top off a bottle of wine. Kim plopped down onto the couch and cried.

"Y'all just don't understand the torture that I has been going through with wanting to give birth to a child," Kim said.

"Girl, we know how hard that was for you," Lele said.

"Y'all really don't. I have been keeping a secret for years that has been eating me alive. I haven't even had enough nerve to tell James," Kim said.

All of the girls sat down to listen because it seemed as if Kim needed to release some stuff.

"Go on, Kim," said Shantel.

"Well, right after I started college, I thought I was in love with this guy. We were inseparable. We talked about getting married and one day having a family. Then one day I found out I was pregnant. The guy denied the baby and broke up with me. He said he wasn't ready to be a father. So, instead of telling my parents or anyone else," she sighed.

"I took out a student loan and paid for an abortion," Kim cried hysterically. "I asked God to forgive me, but I guess he hasn't until now. I felt he had been punishing me all of these years for killing a blessing he was trying to give me. But y'all, I couldn't take care of a baby by myself. I have been lying all of these years saying that I was raped," she lay in Lele's arms.

By the time Kim finished, all of the girls were crying.

"Oh, Kim, it's alright, girl," Lele comforted her.

"Y'all just don't know all of the guilt I have been feeling not being able to give my husband a child. The way he would look at me at times, like something was wrong with me," Kim cried. "Thank you, Jesus, for loving me. Thank you, Jesus, for forgiving me," Kim continued. "It feels so good to be able to talk about it. All of the pain that's been hidden for years doesn't hurt anymore."

"It's amazing that we all can be so close, yet still have those hidden pains," Shantel said. "I have something to share too."

"Uh, before you start, I need to have another drink," Monay laughed, trying to lighten the mood. "I need to grab the tissue from the bathroom too."

Lele continued to rub Kim's back. Monay came back with the whole bottle of wine and issued out toilet tissue to everyone.

"Okay, I'm ready. Go ahead, Shantel."

"Y'all know that my momma was on drugs and that she beat me. Sometimes she beat me just because, but other times was because I didn't want to," Shantel paused and dropped her head.

"Pick your head up, Shantel," Lele said. "We are all here for you. Whatever you need to let go of, now is the time. We can't allow the enemy to torture us any longer with secrets."

"Other times, it was because I refused to have sex with my brother while her boyfriend watched," a tear dropped.

"Whew, that's too much for me," Monay turned up her glass of wine.

After hearing Shantel, Kim dried her tears.

"Y'all can't begin to understand the anger and frustration I have been carrying around all of these years. At times, the pain was just too unbearable. I haven't talked to my brother in years because of it. I know it wasn't either of our faults, but I can't stand to look at him."

No one said anything, but only cried and embraced one another. Then Lele stood up.

"Y'all this is so good for us. Normally I would say stop crying, but I am reminded of something my grandma used to say. She would always tell us that crying was a cleansing time. And at this moment, I feel God cleansing us all," Lele said. "We all sometimes wonder what shapes a person into who they are. We just never know sometimes."

"Amen, Lele," Kim whispered softly.

"I have something I would like to share too, since God is allowing us to have a healing service while on vacation," Lele smiled.

"Wait. I will probably need another drink for this one," Monay said, trying to lighten the mood.

"Pour me one too," Lele said.

"Oh, dang. This has to be serious if little holy roly is going to have a drink," Monay laughed.

"Anyway, Monay. For as long as I can remember you girls have wanted to know why Addai and me got a divorce. Well, I guess there is no better time to tell you than right now. Here goes. I will keep this short. Y'all know I loved Addai more than life itself. I came home early one day and that bastard was doing inappropriate things to my son."

"What does that mean, Lele?" Shantel asked.

"Addai was performing oral sex on Addonte'!"

Shantel dried her tears and all of the girls' mouths dropped.

"Oh, my God, Lele!" Kim said.

"Girl, I am surprised you didn't kill that pervert!" Monay exclaimed.

"What did you do, girl?" Shantel asked.

Lele sat down on the floor and said, "Y'all God had to give me strength because I pulled out my gun. I almost shot him. But aside from all of that, I was devastated."

"Why didn't you ever say anything, Lele?" Kim asked.

"What was I supposed to say? The man I loved has been raping my only child? The pain was too excruciating, and it was so embarrassing for us," Lele explained.

"Wow, Lele," Shantel said.

"That's why you wouldn't give a man the time of day until Darryl came along," Kim said.

"Yes. I wasn't healed, so there was no need to waste my time or anybody else's time. The Lord had to deal with the pain, the guilt, and me. When AD told me he wanted to go away to school, that made me feel even worse. These past years have been lonely and painful, but God has been keeping me," Lele said with excitement. "Y'all don't know how good this feels to be able to talk about it and not feel guilty."

Kim noticed that Monay had started crying. She wondered what was going on with her.

"Monay, what's the matter, boo?" Kim asked.

"Girl, I just can't take all of these confessionals. It's just too much," Monay said.

"This is a good thing, Monay. All of us have been secretly hurting and didn't feel comfortable enough to share with one another. Now God has given us a breakthrough!" Kim rejoiced.

"I guess," Monay said nonchalantly.

"You guess? Monay, what's wrong for real? You can tell us. We're here for you," Shantel said.

"I'm not even sure I can say it," Monay said.

"Just go on and spit it out, girl," Kim urged.

"Since you all have been confessing your inner most secrets, it makes me want to confess mine. Maybe I will feel better too," Monay replied.

"Okay, we're listening," Lele held Monay's hand.

Monay squeezed Lele's hand and mumbled a few words. No one understood what she said.

"Monay, we didn't understand," Lele said.

"I was molested by my stepfather when I was a little girl," Monay admitted.

For a few moments, there was complete silence in the room after she made her confession. Lele hugged

Monay really tight and rubbed her hand gently across her back. Monay cried hysterically.

"Oh, Monay, sweetie, get it all out. Let the Lord heal you," Lele reassured her.

Kim and Shantel walked over to Lele and Monay and shared in a group hug.

"My God, we just never know why people do the things they do," Lele thought to herself.

"Thank y'all so much for being here for me. It really means a lot to me. I have been keeping that secret and vowed to take it to the grave with me," Monay continued.

"Wow, Monay," Shantel said.

"Both my momma and my stepfather were alcoholics. When she would be knocked out cold from her whiskey, he would sneak in my room and fondle me. He would even rub his penis across my vagina. It was horrible. I started sleeping in my clothes for a while. Then my momma caught me and said that was not good hygiene. She just didn't know that I was trying to protect myself. I used to pray, but I guess God didn't hear me. Then one night, I told him with authority, that if he came back, I was going to tell my daddy. I guess he knew I was serious because it stopped. I knew momma wouldn't believe me, so I have never mentioned it."

"Monay, we are so sorry that you had to go through that. But if you really look at it, God did hear your prayer," Lele winked at her.

Monay stood up and said, "Now that I have gotten rid of all of that baggage, I need another drink. Something stronger."

"I guess you will never get delivered from the bottle, huh, lush?" Shantel laughed.

"Y'all now that God has started our healing process; let's keep it going. Of course, we will need to pray and fast to accomplish this mission. After we get home, let's go and face our offenders. It will help us in our healing journey. Then we can help somebody else," Lele recommended.

"Lele, I don't think we are ready for all of that. The first thing I am going to do when I get home is to tell my husband. Then I will tell him our good news!" Kim said.

"I definitely am not ready to see or talk to my momma. All of the hell she has put me through. I need a while for that," Shantel agreed.

"Well, I'm ready when we get back. I want to see my stepdaddy so I can run him over with my car," Monay said.

Kim and Shantel burst out laughing.

"Monay, you are so stupid," Kim said.

"Yet, I am so serious," said Monay.

"Okay, well, maybe not right off, but we need to be working towards that. After I share my story with Darryl, I have to talk to AD. He needs to know that I am planning to go and visit his father in jail. That is going to be extremely difficult," said Lele.

"Girl, you are about to marry Darryl, and he doesn't even know why you are divorced? He is crazy for allowing you to get away with that for so long," Shantel laughed.

"Hey, don't be a hater. I got it like that," Lele giggled.

"Kim, so how are you going to keep your good news a secret for three more days?" Monay asked. "You know you can't hold water good?"

"I'm going to try," Kim smiled.

"You know, I am so glad to have y'all as my friends. We definitely don't agree on everything, and we have our moments, but you have always been there when I needed a friend. Y'all have made my roughest times, not so dreadful. Even when I would go into a shell and shut you all out, you understood. And I know if it weren't for y'all praying me through, I wouldn't have made it. You didn't give up on me. I just want to say thank you," Monay expressed.

"Uh oh, the Lord is on His way back. Monay has had a serious moment," Shantel laughed.

"Girl, that's what friends are supposed to do. We had to love you as a slut and all," Kim laughed so hard she fell to the floor.

"Y'all shut the hell up," Monay cursed. "See, I need to stop fooling with y'all. Y'all will make a sister backslide.

"Not trying to destroy our moment here, but can we order some room service? I'm starving?" Shantel asked.

"Yes, but before we do, let's pray," Lele suggested.

"Holy roly, we can pray after we get our food," Monay said.

"No, we are going to pray now," Lele demanded.

Lele pulled out her oil from her purse and anointed each of them. After they finished praying, they ordered their food and played games.

CHAPTER THIRTEEN

Renewed

The girls sat in the airport waiting to board the airplane so they could head back home. Their plane was delayed because of inclement weather. They were informed that the weather should clear up within the hour and they could leave.

"Y'all, let's go and find us some food. I am hungry. It don't look like the weather is going to clear up anytime soon," Monay said.

"Yes, let's eat. Y'all know I am eating for two now," Kim smiled. "I can't starve my beautiful baby."

"Kim, the baby hasn't even formed yet," Shantel laughed.

"Forget you, Shantel," Kim laughed.

"Shantel, leave Kim alone. We all know that her pregnancy is a miracle, so let her enjoy this time," Lele commented.

"Thanks, Lele, but I am not thinking about that heifer," Kim laughed. "Now, let's find food."

The girls grabbed their valuables and went through the airport looking for a nice restaurant. There wasn't a sit-down restaurant at the airport, so they were forced to eat fast food. The girls ordered their food and sat down in an open food court. After they finished eating, they headed back to their gate and waited.

It wasn't until a few hours had passed that the rain cleared up. The agent came over the intercom, "Attention passengers, flight 0112 will now begin boarding. We apologize for such a lengthy delay, but the weather was out of our control."

All of the anxious passengers shouted with joy.

Monay stood up, "It's about time. They need to get me out of here, or they can put us in a hotel so we can hit the beach. I'm tired of sitting in here. I can't meet any men."

The girls proceeded forward to board the plane.

"I am so glad to be going back home. I can't wait to tell James our good news. Trinitee is about to be a big sister. I pray I am having twins," Kim rejoiced.

"Kim, I am so happy for you. I told you my God would come through if you only believe, trust, and not walk out on your marriage," said Lele.

"I know, girl. I was just so frustrated. I didn't know what else to do."

"Well, now you know, sometimes you just have to wait," Shantel joined the conversation.

"Can y'all just shut up so I can enjoy my flight back. I need to reminisce on all of those Turks men I encountered," Monay fussed.

Then the stewardess announced over the intercom we were about to take off. The girls partied so much, they immediately drifted off to sleep. Three hours had passed when Shantel woke up to the plane swaying from side to side. She noticed out the window it had started raining again. She became quite nervous, so she woke Lele up.

"What is it, Shantel?" Lele whispered.

"Girl, you can't feel the plane dipping and shaking? The weather is really bad out there. Look!"

Lele sat up straight. She leaned in Shantel's lap and stared out of the window. She noticed how bad the weather was. Lele looked around for a flight attendant. She could hear all of the chatter from other passengers. Lele woke Monay and Kim up too.

Before she could flag down a stewardess, the pilot came on over the intercom. "May I have your attention, please? Please fasten your seatbelts and adjust your seats into the upright position. We have extremely high turbulence ahead of us. Please, try to remain calm. Hopefully, it will clear up soon."

Everyone on the plane started talking and the girls became nervous. Kim grabbed her cell phone so she could call James to tell him what was going on. Shantel was already on her phone talking to Gerome.

"Hey, baby," Kim said to James on the phone hysterically.

"Hey, sweetheart. What's going on?" James replied.

"Baby, something is wrong with the plane. We ran into some turbulence. We are so scared, James. I wanted to tell you that I love you," Kim began to cry.

"Kim, calm down. God is not going to take you away from me. I love you too. How are the other girls?" he asked.

"Scared. James, I need to tell you something just in case we crash. I was trying to surprise you until I got home, but I don't know if I am going to make it home," Kim said.

"Kim, don't say that, sweetie."

"Listen, I'm pregnant. We are about to have a baby," her trembling voice spoke.

James started screaming with excitement on the phone.

"Kimmie, that's incredible. God is faithful."

"But what if we don't make it home James?" Kim asked.

"Kimmie, God is not a cruel God. Do you think he would bless us with a baby and then take the two of you away from me? No, he wouldn't?"

"He could have allowed me to get pregnant to show me that He was able before I die." Kim said.

Then Kim heard Lele's phone ringing. It was Darryl. Lele had not called him because she didn't want to alarm him for a little turbulence.

"Kim, Shantel, tell James and Gerome to turn to WTNT. Darryl said it's all over the news. We must really be in trouble," Lele said.

"James, tell Trinitee I love her. Thanks for being such a loving husband. I love you,"
Kim said. "James, the plane is shaking even worst. Pray, baby."

"Kim. Kim. Hello, Kimmie, are you there?" James worried.

They lost their connection. James tried repeatedly but could not get through. He called Darryl and Gerome, but they couldn't get through either.

"I lost my connection. I don't have any bars now," Kim yelled.

"Mine died too," Lele agreed.

The girls asked around, but everyone else had lost service too. Then the lights went out on the plane.

"Passengers, WE CANNOT SEE AHEAD OF US. I REPEAT, WE CANNOT SEE AHEAD OF US. Your oxygen masks are being released. Please place them on your face and ensure your seatbelts are fastened tightly."

Everybody started screaming at once.

"Give me your hands, girls. Lord, in the name of Jesus, I ask that you fix this situation. Keep us in the midst of this storm. Have mercy right now God! Peace be still. Have mercy right now. You have promised us too much and we have lots of kingdom work to do. I know you are not going to take us out like this. I plead the blood of Jesus," Lele prayed.

"God, please help us," Shantel cried.

"Did y'all feel that?" Kim asked.

"It felt like we hit something," Lele said.

"Attention passengers, WE ARE GOING DOWN! I repeat, WE ARE GOING DOWN!" the captain screamed from the cockpit.

Suddenly, the plane dropped from the sky really quickly.

****

Back in the states, Darryl and Gerome had arrived at Kim's house so they could watch the news coverage together. The news anchor reported that the plane had gone down over the Atlantic Ocean, right off the coast of Miami. Diving crews were on the scene trying to rescue anyone they could find alive.

"Man, we need to catch the next plane out of here. The girls need us," James exclaimed.

"James, it's probably best that we stay here until they give us updates on the news," Gerome replied.

Darryl was on the phone with the airlines trying to get some answers. "They said they can't tell us anything right now," he hung up the phone. "The devil is a lie. He will not have my future! We need to get to Miami. I believe God that the girls will be rescued. When they do, I want to be right there!"

"Okay, I will have my mom to meet us at the airport to get Trinitee," James said.

"Fine, let's go. We need to catch the first plane out of here. Gerome, are you coming?" Darryl asked.

"Well, I guess so. Let's go."

****

Back in Miami, the search crews were still rescuing passengers. Lele, Shantel, and Monay walked slowly from the rescue team. Their clothes were baggy and dripped with water. "Y'all where is Kim?" asked Shantel.

"I thought you said everybody was here Monay!" Lele yelled.

"I know I saw Kim," Monay looked all around through the crowd.

Lele tried to run back towards the rescue trucks, but the officers stopped her. "Hey, you have to let me go. Our friend is missing," she cried loudly. "Let me through here. I have to find her!" Shantel and Monay followed her.

One of the officers restrained Lele and asked her nicely to stop yelling. "Ma'am, please just calm down. The search team is doing everything they can to find all of the passengers," the officer said. Then he turned to Shantel and Monay, "I need you ladies to go to the triage area and wait. There is nothing any of us can do now but pray and wait."

"You don't understand, mister. That's my best friend in the entire world. She is missing and she is going to have a baby," Lele's face turned red as she cried.

"Ma'am, please, just go and wait."

Shantel grabbed Lele's hand, "Come on, Lele. Let's do as the man said. We need to go and pray."

Lele stood there with a blank stare.

"Shantel is right. We need to call on our heavenly father right now," Monay agreed.

The girls walked away and sat down in a grassy area.

"I just can't believe this is happening," Lele cried. "After all Kim has been through, Lord, please help Kim. This is all of my fault. We shouldn't have gone anywhere. We should have just celebrated at home."

Shantel lightly slaps Lele. "Girl, snap out of it. Come back to yourself. Now you know none of this is your fault. God allows everything to happen for a reason and you know that, preacher girl."

"Yea, that's right," said Monay.

"Don't you allow the devil to play with your mind right now," Shantel continued.

Then they heard an officer speaking on a bullhorn. "Step out of the way, people. Go back behind this rope. We need to get these people to triage."

The girls stood up, hoping to see Kim with the group of people coming. They stood by franticly waiting for Kim to be rescued.

"Kim! Kim! Where are you?! Kim!" the girls yelled toward the group. Still, there was no response.

CHAPTER FOURTEEN

Not Like This

arryl, James, and Gerome arrive in Miami. They can't get an answer on the girls' cell phones. They hop in a taxi to head to the scene on the beach. There were so many road detours and roadblocks, it took them longer to get there. The police were set up there, so they had to get dropped off as close as they could. They walked the rest of the way.

"Pardon me, gentlemen, you can't go down there," a security officer said.

"To hell we can't. Our wives were on that plane," Gerome replied. The guys broke through the yellow tape onto the beach. One of the news reporters stopped them.

"Excuse me, do you have family down there?" the lady asked.

The guys kept walking, but Darryl stopped.

"Yes, our wives were on that plane. We need to go and find them." Darryl said.

"They are not gonna let you get too far. They have family members hanging over there outside of the triage while they check out all of the passengers." She pointed and continued. "When is the last time you spoke to your wife, sir?"

"Right before the plane went down?"

"Can you tell us what she said happened?"

"No, I cannot. I'm trying to go find her right now," Darryl said and walked away.

The news reporter continued to ask questions and James just shoved the camera out of the way. They headed towards the tents set up. A medic walked up to them.

"Sir, the family area is right over here. You can fill out this paperwork about any family member that was on the plane," the medic said.

"Please forgive me. I don't mean to be rude, but we are not filling out paperwork. We just need to go over here and look for our wives," Gerome said.

"Please, just wait over here. We will be escorting passengers out momentarily so they can call family."

Just then, a group of passengers walked from the tent heading to the family area. Darryl yells.

"Alecia!!! Alecia!! Where are you? Shantel, Kim, Monay!!" yelled Darryl.

"Sir, please stop yelling. That is only gonna cause confusion. Now, go and wait over there!" the medic said sternly.

Darryl yelled again.

"Alecia, Monay, Shantel, Kim!"

As Darryl was yelling, police officers came over to them.

"Sir, I really need you to stop yelling. I understand you are trying to find your family, but we need to keep order," the officer said.

James noticed the officer's chain around his neck and said, "Yo Frat, man we are sorry. We just want to find our wives. Please frat, can you help us?"

The officer gave him the fraternity handshake and a hug. "Yea, man, I'm gonna help you. Who are you looking for?"

"My wife and her 3 friends were on the plane, man. My wife is pregnant," James whimpered.

"Come on. I will take you through the back of the triage to look for them," the officer said.

The officer led them through the crowd towards the back of the triage tent.

"Listen, once you are inside, you can't yell or scream. You have to just walk around to see if you can find them," the officer explained.

"We understand," Gerome said.

They entered the triage and walked around looking for the girls.

Meanwhile, the girls were hugged up together crying and praying. "They need to hurry up and let us make a phone call home," Shantel wept. Lele stopped one of the medics working the triage.

"Ma'am, are they still searching for my friend? My friend is missing?" asked Lele. In a very comforting tone, she said, "Ma'am, yes they are still searching for survivors. Try not to worry."

"Do you have a phone? We need to call home?"

"Phone stations are set up outside. You are in the next group going out," the medic said.

Lele sighed, "Okay."

"This is so screwed up y'all," Monay said.

"I just want my friend back. God, do you hear me? Please send Kim back," Lele whimpered.

"Come on. You all can go now so you can contact your family." The medic ushered them through the front entrance.

****

The fellas continued to look for the girls. By the time they got to the front, the girls had left already.

"Man, they aren't here!" Gerome panicked.

The officer responded, "They are continuously bringing in passengers. Try to stay cool, man."

"That's easier said than done," Darryl said.

The officer led them back outside. As they walked over to the holding area, Darryl and Gerome's phones rang. Gerome tried to answer his, but he couldn't get it out of his backpack before it stopped ringing. Darryl's was easily accessible to him in his back pocket.

"Hello? Hello?!" Darryl said.

"Darryl, it's me! It's me. We can't find Kim," she cried.

Darryl turned to James and Gerome, "It's Alecia! They're alive! They're alive!"

Gerome and James did a praise dance right there on the scene.

"Alecia, baby, calm down. I can't understand what you are saying. Where are you?"

"I don't know where we are. It's crowded, the news people are here. We can't find Kim," she continued.

"Listen, we are on the scene in Miami. I just need to find you," Darryl explained.

"You're gonna have to help me get to you. What do you see from where you are?"

"Behind us is the big white tent where they have all of the passengers that were on the plane."

Darryl interrupted her. "We just left from there. Go back to the tent and we will meet you there."

"But, Darryl, we can't find Kim," Lele said.

"Just go back to the tent. We are on our way."

The guys hurried back towards the tent.

****

"Come on y'all! The guys are here, and they are meeting us at the tent. How are we gonna tell James that we lost Kim?" asked Lele.

"I don't know," Shantel said.

The girls hurried back to the tent. As they were walking in, they heard someone yelling Lele's name. They turned around and saw Darryl, James, and Gerome coming towards them. Lele ran to Darryl and squeezed him so tight. Shantel did the same to Gerome.

"Lele, where is Kim?" James asked.

Lele cried again. She took James by the hand and said, "James, I'm so sorry. We lost Kim! We lost Kim!"

"What do you mean you lost Kim, Lele?! She is your best friend! You were supposed to take care of her. She's pregnant for God's sake," James screamed at her. Then he turned to Monay and Shantel. "How could y'all do this?"

"I'm sorry, James. I'm sorry," Lele cried.

Gerome said, "Calm down, James. I'm sure they are gonna find her."

"Lele, what happened, baby?" Darryl asked.

"We were all holding hands, but then the plane crashed in the water. They managed to open the doors and we grabbed our seats so we could float. Then we left the plane together. We were just trying to stay alive. But there was so much debris and people everywhere. Rescue boats were out grabbing anybody that they could and we all were separated. It wasn't until we made it back to land that we realized that Kim was no longer with us," Lele said.

Then James fell to his knees. Darryl and Gerome picked him up, trying to console him. As they were standing there, another group of passengers were coming in with the rescue crews. They didn't see Kim in that group either walking in the tent.

"Help me. Y'all gotta help me find Kim! She's about to have our baby," James said.

"We are gonna find her James," said Lele. Just then, they see people being brought up from the water on stretchers. Then Shantel notices the shirt Kim was wearing hanging from one of the stretchers. She screamed. "Y'all there's Kim!" They try to run towards them, but they are stopped again.

James angrily said, "Listen, I think that's my pregnant wife they are taking to the ambulance. I need to go check. Please let me go check." Just then, his frat brother ran over and told security he would escort him over to see if that was his wife. His frat told him that one more person could come with them.

"Lele, I think you should go," said Monay.

With tears still rolling down her face, she agreed. Darryl hugged Lele and she walked with James and his frat brother. As they got closer, the paramedics were closing the door.

"Wait! I need to see if that's my wife," James said. The paramedics explained to him they needed to get that patient to the hospital.

"Please, sir!!" Lele yelled.

The paramedic opened the door back and it was Kim laying there unconscious.

"Kimmie!!!!! Noooo!!! My wife!" He jumped in the back of the ambulance. "Lele, meet us at the hospital."

The paramedics closed the door and then they drove off. Lele ran back to the others.

"Y'all, it's Kim," she cried. "She is unconscious. She is not awake y'all. We gotta pray. We gotta get to the hospital!"

"How are we gonna get there?" Shantel asked.

"Hell, let's hitch hike a ride or steal a car. Either way, let's go," Monay said.

They ran up to the street and saw an SUV waiting with an UBER sticker in the window. Monay knocked on his window to ask for a ride, but he said he was waiting on someone. She grabbed him by his face and gave him a sloppy kiss. The driver was so shocked, he told them to just jump in. He put his hazard lights on and sped to the hospital. They jumped out and ran inside. James was sitting in the emergency room.

"James, how is Kim?" Darryl asked.

"She's in emergency surgery. They don't know if she and the baby are gonna make it," he cried. "I can't lose her."

"You won't, man," Gerome said.

A couple of hours passed by when the doctor came out to give them an update. The doctor explained that

Kim was in a coma and the baby still had a heartbeat. He was still unsure if they were gonna make it.

"If they come out of this, it will definitely be a miracle. I'm sorry," the doctor explained. "You all can go in for a few minutes to visit, and then only her husband can stay." Then he left. Everyone was crying and in total disbelief. They all went to Kim's room and just stood there crying. As Darryl prayed, James laid down across Kim's body in tears.

KIA STOKES

Acknowledgements

HONORING my husband, Taronta Stokes, who has encouraged and selflessly supported me in every endeavor and vision given by God. I honor you as a man of God, my ribcage, husband, covering, and best friend. Thanks for being my number one tumbler.

ACKNOWLEDGING my daughter, Trinitee Stokes(my MEGASTAR). Mommy loves you and always remember that you are the apple of God's eye!

SPECIAL THANKS:

God and his infinite power, my mother (Annie Allen), father (Arthur Torrance), Tosha Moore, Lynda "Faye" Rice, Brian & Stacey Donaldson, Bishop & 1ST Lady Jakes, Minister Grace Walker, Darryl & Rhonda Garrett, Dr. Tongie Scott, Torri Powell, Minister Karen Courts, Felicia Brookins, and Bobby Quillard Photography.

Author's Bio

Kia Stokes was born and raised in Jackson, MS. She resides in Los Angeles, CA with her husband, Taronta and daughter, Trinitee. With an Economics degree from Tougaloo College, and an M.B.A. from Jackson State University, most people are often astonished with her writing and acting abilities. Known for having such a witty spirit, she is often told that she attended college for the wrong major.

Although Kia suffered several tragedies during her childhood, including sexual abuse, God has allowed her to rise above the hurt and turn the pain into power. He has brought her from tragedy to triumph. After the storm, God anointed her with unspeakable joy in her life and the gift to usher joy into the lives of others through writing and her mere presence. Her literary mission is to address real-life issues with a touch of spiritual humor.

Her work will demonstrate and promote the importance of salvation, healing, deliverance, the power of forgiveness, unconditional love and healthy relationships.

Kia has traveled with Gospel stage plays where she had leading roles and have also written and directed short plays. She is the author of UNBOUND, which has also been adapted to the movie FORGIVENESS starring Richard T. Jones.

She spends most of her time with her loving husband, bonding with her daughter, family, friends, and serving the community. Kia is also a member of Alpha Kappa Alpha Sorority, Inc.

Connect with Kia Stokes

Thanks for your purchase!

For bulk orders of books and to purchase t-shirts
and other merchandise go to www.kiastokes.com

Reviews, questions & concerns contact with
Kia Stokes via email kiastokes1908@gmail.com
Instagram at @kiastokes1908

Looking forward to connecting with you!